PENGUIN BOOKS

C2126

TAKE ONLY AS DIRECTED

JAMES BYROM

James Byrom was born in Edinburgh in 1911 and spent much of his early youth in the Highlands. After leaving Oxford, he worked on the *London Mercury* under Sir John Squire. During the thirties he published his first five books and travelled, in the steps of Evelyn Waugh, to Abyssinia. During and after the war he also travelled widely, under the patronage of the Finland Fund, the British Council, and the Royal Army Medical Corps. The latter guided him through Normandy, the Ardennes, and Germany, giving him a pleasantly idle spell in Palestine to round off the war. All this he described in his autobiography *The Unfinished Man* (1957).

Since retiring, twelve years ago, from teaching English literature at Helsinki University, he has lived on a small property in the south of France, writing, making wine, and taking things rather too easily for spiritual comfort. After three crime books he doubts if crime pays, and has – at least temporarily – tried to 'go straight'. Another crime novel by James Byrom, *Or Be He Dead*, is also available in Penguins.

James Byrom

TAKE ONLY
AS DIRECTED

Penguin Books

in association with Chatto & Windus

Penguin Books Ltd, Harmondsworth, Middlesex, England
Penguin Books Pty Ltd, Ringwood, Victoria, Australia

—

First published by Chatto & Windus 1959
Published in Penguin Books 1964

—

—

Made and printed in Great Britain
by Hunt, Barnard & Co. Ltd,
Aylesbury
Set in Monotype Baskerville

Contents

Chapter 1

The Lights Turn Red

On our sixth wedding anniversary Sally said casually: 'David, what day is it?'

'Wednesday – my worst day in the week.'

'Yes, but Wednesday *October the second* – do you remember? ... I've got tickets for the Criterion tonight.'

I shook my head over my lapse, and Sally said anxiously: 'Please don't tell me you're expecting again?'

'As a matter of fact I *am* expecting, but since the baby's already a week overdue, it can surely wait a few more hours.'

The play was about a high-minded doctor who put his work before his wife and was finally brought to heel by her elopement with a fictive sculptor, a passionate and ruthless man. But when I accused Sally of getting at me unfairly, she pretended to be astonished: 'Did you really think those people were like us?'

After the play we went to supper at the Berkeley. Then on to a nightclub called The Secret Rose. There, she assured me, we would be able to feel unmarried again, thus reliving the courtship she nostalgically recalled as 'short and vicious'.

I used to be light on my feet playing racquets. But then I had my hands to think about. When I dance I am always haunted by the image of frail, silken barques being pursued and rammed by pilotless patent-leather battleships. The reckless speed of the waltz makes my lower members behave as though unstrung by locomotor ataxy. I was trying to obey Sally's instructions to 'relax and listen to the music', when somebody tapped me on the shoulder. Clinging to Sally I came to a standstill. And when my head stopped going round, there was Pat, grinning at me with half-closed eyes and wide half-open mouth. Her chin, with its shadow of a cleft, rested on the shoulder of her partner, who was young, tall and willowy; with a great deal of neck hair.

'Hullo, David,' she said, 'hullo, Sally. Come and join us after this. We're sitting over there under the band.' An emerald lit up as she waved her hand, and her smooth brandy-coloured hair, falling over white naked shoulders, seemed to burn for a moment as it was whirled away on the dim turbulence of faces.

Sally said: 'She looks lovely, less debauched than I've ever seen her. After two divorces – or is it three – I suppose she's beginning to know what she wants. . . .'

We danced on in silence till the band stopped. Then Sally said: 'Let's go and join them, shall we?'

I felt sure she didn't really want to. Though I hadn't seen much of Pat in recent years, outside professional visits, Sally never forgot that Pat and I had grown up together.

'Doesn't Pat seem a bit irrelevant on our wedding anniversary?' As soon as I had said it, I realized that the anniversary was precisely what made Pat relevant. She was a reagent for testing our marriage, and if Sally resented her, she was also attracted by her.

Sally smiled ingenuously up at me: 'She's got a new man and I don't like being out of date!'

'*Plus ça change*,' I said, tightening my grip on Sally's appreciable waist.

'This is Paul Latta . . . Doctor and Mrs Mortimer.'

'Ha-ju-doo' – the voice confirmed my impression that Pat's taste hadn't wavered. From Dickie Syme, the band-

THE LIGHTS TURN RED

leader, to Lord Killaloe, they had all been in their element in
night clubs, and this one conformed so perfectly to the pattern
that I saw him as a figure in a modern decorative composi-
tion: the pose elegant, the face absolutely blank.

'Paul, get another bottle. This is a celebration.'

I didn't like to ask what there was to celebrate. But by way
of finding out I raised my glass: 'Well, here's to us all. Do you
realize, Pat, that Sally and I have been married six years
today?'

'*No, really!* It seems only yesterday that I disgraced myself
by getting pickled at your wedding. When I think of all *my*
marital antics, the tightrope walking and the somersaults' –
she laughed wildly and then went into a fit of asthmatic
coughing. 'My God,' she gasped, 'it's all too much . . .
Paul, feel in my bag and get out that little bottle of blue
pills.'

Master Latta obeyed, looking bewildered, and Pat took
one with a gulp of whisky. 'Thank you, darling. David, do
you remember when you were a student, how you used to
feed me like a sick canary with tiny white ephedrine pills?'
She grimaced at herself in her hand-mirror, sticking out a
tongue that aroused my professional interest. 'What a wreck I
am! I don't know how Paul can bear to take me out dancing,
let alone . . . ' – her hand, white and exquisite with its single
emerald and five rubies of lacquer, rested teasingly on Latta's
– 'let alone want to *marry* me!'

Latta giggled and, leaning over behind Pat, bit her fondly
on the shoulder-blade. Sally and I exchanged glances, and at
that moment the band struck up again. The bass player, who
had been drinking in our conversation, grinned vacantly
down upon us from the platform, alternately plucking and
whacking his giant instrument in what was apparently a
private serenade.

I said: 'Come on, Pat, let's dance.'

'Well, what do you think of Paul?'

'I should think he performs very well as long as there's an organ grinding nearby.'

'Then you don't think I ought to marry him? Aren't you being insular?'

'Be serious, Pat. After two marriages, you must have learnt *something* about yourself.'

'I have. That's why I've decided to get married again. That's why I said it was a celebration.'

'But you can't. You simply can't go on playing the fool. Is there nothing short of illness that will preserve you from yourself?'

She looked up at me and laughed gaily: 'Dear David, always the same medical and spiritual adviser. It's such heaven to tease you, I really can't help myself.'

'You mean you're not going to marry this Paul?'

'Of course not. I may be neurotic, but I'm not completely bats. Actually, tonight's my farewell to the life I've been leading. I just wanted one last wallow, so as to get the habit right out of my system. That's why I chose Paul. He's kept by an elderly divorcee who passes as his mother. Being bitten by him is the most immunizing experience a loose woman can have. But to give him his due, he's a divine dancer; and he really is very fond of me.'

'Then you're not going to marry anybody?'

She nodded against my chest. 'I'm going to marry a man called Dugald McBane who farms cattle out in Kenya. As soon as my decree becomes absolute, that is. He was a war-hero and he's got a good poker-faced sense of humour.'

'And then you're going to live in Kenya?' The idea of Pat disappearing out of my life was surprisingly difficult to bear.

'Dugald tells me disillusioned peeresses make excellent pioneeresses. And you said yourself I ought to get out of England and live in a dry healthy climate with a strong silent man who wants children. What was the phrase you used? – "Your sort of asthma's an alarm bell; when you hear it you've got to change your way of life." '

'I didn't mean you had to tear yourself up by the roots; that could be traumatic. Did you meet him when you were out there this spring?'

'No, he picked me up on the ship coming home. I'd been having a succession of parties in Nairobi, and I was feeling remote and unapproachable. So I couldn't help noticing Dugald, who also looked remote and unapproachable, and ... well, a few nights before we docked at Southampton, there was one of those macabre fancy-dress affairs and he and I were the only ones under seventy who hadn't bothered to dress up, and oddly enough we had both gravitated to the bar. I was vaguely watching the revelry through the bar door, feeling what they call "social pressure", when I heard a deep Scotch voice booming in my ear: "I'm looking for somebody human. Do you happen to be human by any chance?" ... David, I was enchanted. He had expressed exactly how I was feeling. What's more he didn't try and make a pass at me. From that moment on we were soul-mates.'

'Hmm,' I said, 'you seem to have broken new ground.'

'I've never met anybody like him. He's lonely and dis-enchanted and a bit antisocial, but somehow – oh, well, you'll see ...'

I said: 'What's made him disenchanted – life in Kenya?'

'That's part of it. He thinks the socialists in Parliament are trying to stab the Kenya settlers in the back. It must be pretty sickening to hear politicians waffling about Habeas Corpus and self-determination for the Kikuyu, when you're sitting up night after night with a gun, watching the door and listening; when you know that these people have drunk human blood and sworn to butcher all the settlers.'

I said: 'Yes, that must be bitter. Clearly Kenya's no place for you at the moment.'

'But if I'm not with him, I'm absolutely nowhere, and he's got his livelihood to defend. Besides, he really needs me. Since his wife ratted on him five years ago, he's had no woman in his life but Nairobi casuals. His emotional life seems to have been mainly centred on the snow-capped peak of Mount Kenya. He can see it, thirty miles away, glittering in the moonlight like a goddess.'

'He sounds disenchanted about women too. How come he needs you so badly when he was getting on so well with Mount Kenya?'

Pat stopped dead in the middle of the dance-floor, digging her long nails into the palm of my hand. People looked at us curiously. 'What's the matter with you, David? Surely it's a bit late in the day to be jealous.' She had always been aware of the annihilating effect of declaiming private lines publicly.

I said, 'I'm not jealous: I'm concerned about you and I thought you were consulting me.'

At that moment I saw Sally. She had been just behind us, and Pat, no doubt, had been aware of it. Her body, for all its weight, was dancing with ease and grace, but her eyes rested on me anxiously. Latta, feeling that she wasn't quite with him, gyrated quickly, billowing her round him like a blue cape. As they danced away, his face was a mask of false ecstasy.

'If I were McBane,' I said, 'I'd leave you in London in the care of armed eunuchs.'

I had left my car at home. So Pat, after dropping Latta surprisingly close to Westminster Cathedral, drove us home to Hans Crescent. It was a blustering autumn night. The last leaves, looking strangely alive in the lamplight, were being torn from the plane-trees in Eaton Square and chased along in scattering droves. Pat too seemed more driven than driving, at the mercy of some inner equinox. She drove with such terrifying caprice that Sally, who was sitting with her, could hardly summon up the necessary monosyllables to punctuate the flow of chatter: Pat was the sort of girl who never talks seriously with women. As I drowsed off she was telling Sally how to prevent the London atmosphere from ruining her complexion, which, after four years of London life, was as near perfection as possible. . . .

There was a scream of brakes and I was jolted violently forward, hitting my forehead on a metal ashtray. For a fleeting second, before I became aware of the red traffic-light glaring officiously over Pat's high shoulder, I thought we had had an accident. I had a strange sensation that this sudden check to our career through space had projected me forward out of my body. I was floating onwards with Sally and Pat, on up a wide empty highway, wrapped in a caul of light. . . .

Then Pat began to express her impatience by treading on the accelerator.

As we were saying good night, Pat said to me: 'When can I bring Dugald to see you? . . . David, what *have* you done to your head?'

'I ran it against a brick wall! What about Friday after dinner? Is that okay, Sally?'

'Yes, of course.' She gave me one of her martyred looks. 'It's okay for *us*, but Pat's always booked up in the evenings.'

Pat said: 'If Sally doesn't want me I *could* be engaged. Actually Friday happens to be the opening of the new Chinchilla Club. But I'm a reformed character from now onwards. It's a great help that Dugald hates dancing. Shall we come about nine?'

On Friday evening I was delayed at the London Clinic. One of my few genuine patients, a disobedient financier, had worn through his duodenum; and Galbraith, called from his club to operate, seemed to think it was all my fault. He always thought it was somebody's fault, a deliberate sabotage of the delicate machine. His enemies were never tired of telling about the occasion when, in the heat of the theatre, his glasses slipped off the end of his nose, and fell into the vitals of the Home Secretary. Now he handled the financier's intestine like an overworked grandmother darning a stocking for a sluttish parent. 'Tcha!' he kept exclaiming testily, looking up from his work to shake his head at me. '*Tripes à la mode*, Dr Mortimer, *tripes à la mode*.' Afterwards, when we were disrobing, he said: 'It'll be his liver next; you'll see. The trouble with you physicians is that bedside manner. You should show 'em the instruments of torture, scare the daylights out of 'em.'

'If we did,' I retorted, 'we'd be out on the streets, and you'd be cutting up meat at Smithfield market.'

During the delicate stitchery at the end, I had stopped admiring Galbraith's skill and started wondering about McBane. From what Pat had told me I pictured him as grizzled, with a hooked nose and theodolite eyes, and with big battered hands he wouldn't know what to do with in a drawing-room.

My first glimpse of him made me suspect one of Pat's social jokes. He had the body of an athlete, with brown curly hair and eyes that disappeared in strong light like the young Lindberg's in the photographs. He didn't look a day older than thirty-five. In his 'sports jacket', corduroys and turtleneck sweater, relaxing in an armchair with his feet crossed on the fender, he might have been one of those horsy young bloods lured out to Kenya after the war by government promises of a land flowing with peanut butter and gold. My heart sank. But as soon as he stood up to greet me, I saw that his clothes were brand new and off the peg. He was wearing the uniform of careful casualness imposed by Regent Street outfitters on every overseas visitor who didn't want to look foreign or colonial. He would have looked more at ease, I thought, in shorts and a bush-shirt.

His handshake was reassuring. And when he opened his mouth my first impression was completely erased. The Scotch Rs, slightly blurred by some impediment, gave his voice a pleasantly outlandish timbre, which explained Pat's reactions meeting him on the boat. When I was telling them about Galbraith I noticed that his facial muscles didn't respond like Pat's and Sally's to the ordinary social stimuli: he didn't care whether I thought he was amused or not: but he followed me politely, nodding an occasional grave 'uh-hah' which I found rather putting-off.

'Well, David,' he said, when I had finished – Pat had refused to let him call me 'Doc' because that somehow reminded her of 'Quack' – 'maybe our witch-doctors aren't so out-of-date after all. They scare their patients by wearing masks. And what's more, they reckon to cure without surgery. Did you ever see a Loch Fyne herring cured? . . . Nor did I; but they tell me it's all done by smoke.'

Pat giggled. 'White man's medicine all-de-same no damn good. When I get to this godforsaken place Bwala I shall hire myself the best wizard in the district.' She clapped her thumbs to the top of her head, spreading her fingers up like antlers; then, with green eyes rolling, she danced forward into the room with high-speed catlike steps. '*Ai bwana, panga,*' she chanted, '*Ai, bwana, panga, ai ai.*'

She sat down amid applause from Sally and me. But Dugald wasn't amused. He was gazing into the fire, pulling at the lobe of his right ear. 'Pat's taking the mike out of me,' he said, 'because she thinks I take the witch-doctor too seriously. But there's no other way to take him nowadays. In Kenya he's a powerful political instrument. He's behind the oath-taking ceremonies that are making killers out of decent boys by de-grading them till they feel outcasts from society, till they're ready to butcher women and children. I happened on one of these oath-taking ceremonies in a cowman's *boma* on my ranch . . . ' He broke off, puffed his cigarette, and added: 'But I expect you've heard all this from newspapers or from friends out in the colony?'

I said: 'No, I haven't. Do go on.'

'No, *don't* go on,' Pat said suddenly. I noticed that her eyes were apprehensive, the eyes of an asthmatic on the verge of an attack. 'Do you know why Dugald's telling all this, Sally? He thinks he'll get David to gang up with him and stop me sailing on November 2nd. But it won't work, Dugald and David! I've had enough of being a war-wife and I'm going *with* Dugald or not at all . . . My God, it's stuffy in this room. Can't somebody open a window?'

I opened a window, while Pat unobtrusively swallowed a pill. Dugald helped himself to another drink. Then he went over to Pat and sat down on the arm of her chair: 'All right, Patricia, we won't quarrel about it any more.' His hand touched her ear and pulled gently at the lobe. 'You know, I used to think I was tough. But it seems I'm not tough enough to keep both you and Mau Mau away from Bwala. What do you think, David? Will she stand the life?'

'She'll stand anything that doesn't frustrate her desires. She could blackmail St Jerome with that asthma of hers. Thank heaven she's going to be your problem from now onwards – yours and the witch-doctor's.'

'Well,' he said, 'I'm a pretty good cow-doctor. I reckon I can handle her.'

Pat lay back on his arm, relaxed again. 'You can't start too soon,' – she closed her eyes, smiling, and ran her tongue over her upper lip – 'it's a pity about that damned Decree Absolute.'

'When do you get your Absolution?' Sally asked. She had a soft sentimental look, but I couldn't resist the thought that she would feel safer with Pat married off in Kenya.

'In two weeks' time. If all goes according to plan, we shall get married just before we sail. I shall be wearing a topee trimmed with mosquito netting and Dugald will be carrying a Colt. Will you and David be witnesses?'

Chapter 2

Faithlessly Fraternal

THEY left soon afterwards, about midnight. Sally and I, standing at the open window, watched them emerge, arm-in-arm, and get into Pat's car. They didn't drive away immediately, and Sally said: 'I think they really are in love. I do hope she'll let him wear the trousers.'

I said: 'She'll fight the sex-war till she knows she's beaten, then she'll worship him for ever more. I imagine he won't give way so easily once he's on his own ground. *I* wouldn't have given in over this Kenya business.'

Sally laughed. 'Oh yes, you would! Do you remember how you gave in about premarital love as soon as I sat on your Anglican scruples? – And I wasn't such a fat girl then!'

'If I had any scruples, I certainly don't remember you sitting on them. You must have been a good shock-absorber, even then. Well, what do you think of Dugald?'

'He's the sort of man I would want to marry if I were Pat – strong, safe, dependable, and wholly male.'

'A bit too self-contained, I would have thought. Despite what she says about being needed. But promising – yes, promising.'

Twelve hours later I was sitting in my car, stuck fast in a block of lunch-hour traffic, when black headlines pounced at me out of a yellow ground.

PEERESS FINDS OLD NURSE BATTERED TO DEATH
BY JEWEL-THIEF

I wasn't interested in peeresses as such. Nor in violence for

18

mercenary motives. What induced me to shout for a midday paper was the other headline:

FLYING SAUCER LANDS ON DARTMOOR?

I had a slight hangover, rarefied by the ether I had been breathing; and I was just in the mood for science fiction.

' 'Ere you are, Guv – ' a wolfish face was framed by the window – 'I reckon diamonds is fair game. But for the job on the old girl the rope's too easy.'

'Good for you!' I said vaguely. 'Keep the change.' Then my eye, skimming the fresh, hairy newsprint, suddenly tripped over a name – the romantic style Pat had been wearing for the last three seasons and was about to discard for plain Mrs McBane.

'The Countess of Killaloe, beautiful thirty-year-old former wife of Dickie Syme, the dance-band leader, came in from a party at four this morning. Her foster-mother, Mrs (Johnny) Tatham, with whom she is at present living, left town on Friday for her country house, taking with her all the servants except Annie Bligh, formerly Lady Killaloe's nurse and for many years housekeeper at No 10 Ovington Square. Lady Killaloe, who sleeps on the second floor, went to bed without noticing anything unusual. At eight o'clock she was awake again and went down to the basement to make tea. At the foot of the stairs, in the passage between the kitchen and the servants' hall, she found the old woman lying in a pool of blood: she had been savagely and repeatedly struck on the head by an unidentified blunt instrument. Jewellery to the value of £5,000 is missing from the house and it is thought that she surprised the thief as he was. . . .'

A blaring of motor horns behind me. I let in my clutch with such a jerk that I stalled the motor. At that moment a taxi squeezed in between me and the road-island. 'Who do you think you are?', a furious voice shouted in my ear, 'a fuggin mobile municipal reading-room?'

But the voice hardly penetrated. As I drove on I was listening to an inner voice, the voice of Annie Bligh telling Pat: *You wouldn't have messed up your life, my dear, if you hadn't been so keen on growing out of David. He was the only one that understood you.* Poor Nanny. She had always been my ally, ever since the day when Pat and I had been caught kissing in the shrubbery during one of Mrs Tatham's county tennis parties. 'Bless their hearts,' she had told Pat's foster-mother. 'Pat's an attractive little minx – why deny it? But David's got his head screwed on all right and it'll take more than a couple of kisses to loosen it.'

I drew up at Hans Crescent and plunged into the mausoleum I had inherited with my uncle's practice. Llewellyn materialized in the hall as the coffin-like grandfather clock knelled the quarter. He was rubbing his hands in the way that always reminded me he had once been employed in a Mental Hospital where one of the inmates had died of cold. Llewellyn was also part of my heritage, the maggot in the rosy windfall.

'Lady Killaloe is here, Sir. I *put* her in the drawing-room.'

'Of course. Did you give her a drink?'

'I thought she looked as if she had had enough. She seemed, if I may say so, a bit unsteady.'

'IDIOT!' – I had been trying for months to provoke Llewellyn into giving notice.

I needn't have worried about drinks. Pat had helped herself to neat whisky. By a miracle of make-up she had managed to conceal the darkness under her eyes, but the skin looked rough, and she had dropped ash down her neat black suit. She saw the newspaper in my hand.

'It's so awful, David, I still can't believe it's true. Why Nanny, of all people in the world? The only comfort I can find is that she couldn't have *known* anything about it. They say she must have been hit from behind just as she reached the bottom of the stairs. She must have heard something and come down to investigate. . . . Oh God, I'm so tired.' She threw her cigarette into the fireplace and lit another with shaking hand. 'If it hadn't been for Dugald, I don't know what I would have done. He rang up Mummy in the country; he got on to Annie's sister in Ealing; he helped me cope with the police. He's so calm and strong. . . .'

'But what can *I* do, Pat? What have you come to see *me* about?'

The note of injury didn't escape her. 'But David, I've been trying to get you all the morning, chasing you vainly from clinic to clinic. At the London Clinic they said you were in the theatre. . . . As a matter of fact you *can* do something, something I wouldn't think of asking anybody else in the whole world. . . .'

'Well?' I asked suspiciously.

She took a gulp of whisky, then a deep breath: 'The detective who questioned me this morning was quite civil and sympathetic in a forbidding way, though he obviously regarded me as cretinous. But it's those damned reporters, David – they've been buzzing round me like bluebottles round a piece of rare steak. One of them, not content with my statement that I got in at four this morning, had the nerve to ask me where I'd been! When I answered vaguely that I'd been with friends, he wanted to know what friends. He made no bones about his motive for asking. A crime like this is hot news, he said. But when it happens in the home of a peeress who's divorcing her husband, the public wants a *social slant* as well. Imagine! To cut a long story short, I panicked – I lied about where I had been between twelve and four this morning – I said I was having drinks with you and Sally! You can guess where I was really?'

'With Dugald at his hotel?'

'No, that would have been dangerous. We were at Cynthia Andrei's flat, which I always use when I want to be private. You see, if that little item came out, my divorce from Desmond would be wrecked. And you know what that means to me now?'

I considered for a moment, then I asked: 'Did you tell the police that too?'

'I believe I did . . . well, I had to be consistent, didn't I? . . . Now please, David, I can't bear it if you start disapproving. After all, this isn't the first time I've asked you to connive, and there's nothing actually *immoral* about it, is there?' She gazed at me with round eyes that looked almost violet in their pale setting, against the coppery lights of her hair.

'Of course there's nothing immoral about it.' – How could I expect her to see the irony of asking *me* to provide her with sexual alibis? I was so safely, so faithfully fraternal. And nowadays I had the additional advantage of being the family doctor, solidly married and accepted – even by the redoubtable Mrs Tatham – as a good influence in Pat's life.

I said: 'Now listen, Pat. What you don't seem to realize is that this isn't the usual, casual alibi. This one has to stand up to publicity, to satisfy the curiosity of any enemies you may have, potential agents of the Queen's Proctor. Is anybody interested in stopping your divorce?'

'Yes, of course, Desmond himself is interested, now he's got rid of his Windmill girl. He pretends that was never serious and he's furious with me because I won't play any more. He practically threatened to put detectives on me: that's why I went back to live at Ovington Square.'

'Hm,' I said, 'lucky the street was empty when you left last night. Llewellyn's the only possible snag, but he sleeps like the log he is. Madhouse keepers couldn't stick the job if they didn't spend at least ten hours plunged in triassic mindlessness.'

'Then it's all right? . . . David, you're sweet, taking all this so calmly and efficiently. Actually I hardly knew what I was doing or saying. The shock of coming down and finding Nanny, when I had woken up feeling so wonderful about Dugald and life in general . . . you know what Nanny meant to me, what she'll always mean. . . . '

'She was the only mother you ever had.'

'You remember how it was when I was thirteen, with a spotty face and scurfy hair? Mummy couldn't bear to look at me. She couldn't parade me any more in public. But nothing ever made any difference to Nanny. She coped with the spots, the self-conscious squirmings and the awkwardness, and she stood up unflinchingly to my searching sex-quizzes, though – poor darling – she couldn't have known a thing about it. And later, when I came to realize my power over men, she was always on my side, however badly I behaved. . . . Oh Nanny, Oh darling Nanny . . . '

Suddenly she looked red and shiny as she used to when her pony hadn't been groomed properly and the dust made her weep and sneeze. I put out my hand and stroked her hair. Diffidently. She had always been taboo, one way or another.

She looked at me for a moment as though she didn't see me at all. Then she buried her head in my lap and the sofa shook with her passionate sobbing.

I stroked her hair and said nothing. It was coarse, sensuous hair – her mother's, I had always assumed. It was fascinating to speculate that her mother could have been one of those raddled red-headed females lurking in strategic doorways just out of the stare of Piccadilly Circus. That thought made me stroke her hair against the grain. I was looking for the little white scar the flint had made when, unbearably teased about one of my father's Sunday sermons, I had pushed her backwards off a stile. . . .

The door opened and Sally stood there looking on. Pat felt me stiffen and raised her head. Then she got up quickly and started repairing her face in the mirror over the mantelpiece.

I picked up the newspaper and handed it to Sally in silence. All that could be said by way of explanation was written there in black and white. . . .

Chapter 3

The Hammer of the House

SALLY really was a shock-absorber. She took the jolt for all of us without showing any signs of strain herself. She thumbed her way quickly through the newspaper column, while we watched her anxiously. Then she went over to Pat and put her arm round her shoulders: 'I know there's nothing I can say that David hasn't said already ... but if there's anything in the world either of us can *do*? ...'

And she so obviously meant it that Pat said, with equal sincerity: 'Just go on being a wonderful friend, Sally. I think I'm going to need wonderful friends.'

She walked out without another word.

Associated with the various crises in my life, there is always a cold lunch, waiting to be eaten without appetite, to induce the flat realistic mood that follows emotional expense. I think it was more to convince *myself* of the disinterestedness of my behaviour with Pat that I pushed aside a plate of cold beef and said: 'You know, I wouldn't put it past Pat to have had that alibi in mind when she arranged to bring Dugald to see us.'

'That's petty, David, as well as unlikely. Anyway, what if she did? Have you forgotten how it was before we were married? – the awful anticlimax of having to say goodnight on the steps of some dreary hotel in Great Russell Street? The way things happened, I consider she was perfectly right to use us – she stood to lose Dugald – no less. Time is death when you're thirty and in love. After all, we're not risking much.'

By the time we had finished lunch, the second patient had already arrived, and Llewellyn could be heard from the waiting-room ostentatiously sympathizing with the first one: I'm afraid we're a bit late starting this afternoon, sir. The doctor had *company*, which made him late for his lunch.'

He was my most tiresome patient, the last and craziest of the wealthy valetudinarians on whom my uncle had constructed his prosperous practice. I had weaned him away from his gastric ulcer by sending him to swallow barium and rubber tubing at a hospital. I had found no other way of exploding the myth of disseminated sclerosis but by threatening him with a lumbar puncture. Now he had been reading up about his bile-duct, and he had brought two test-tubes containing excretions, neatly labelled and sealed with tartan scotch tape.

'I know you, doctor,' he said accusingly, as soon as I showed signs of impatience. 'You're an optimist. You'll never be the physician your uncle was, because you're practically a Christian Scientist: you don't respect your patients until they're dying. But you won't get me, young man. If you don't do something this time, I'll go and get a second opinion.' He had often had second opinions, and each time they had confirmed mine.

'You could get another doctor,' I said.

At that moment there was a knock on the door and Llewellyn put his skull-like head round it, waggling his eyebrows significantly.

'What is it, Llewellyn?' I asked sharply.

'A patient, sir, who *needs urgent attention*.'

'What's the matter? This isn't a casualty ward.'

'I'm afraid I can't say.' And then, having succeeded in suggesting some *louche* contact, if not with Abortion, at least with Drugs: 'I think this card will make it plain, sir.'

I read: *Chief-Inspector Buxton. Criminal Investigation Department. New Scotland Yard.*

This was too much. The sight of my valetudinarian methodically stripping off cardigans provoked a mild recrudescence of that unpleasant dissecting-room humour I hadn't indulged since student days. 'Stop,' I said. 'In your delicate condition there's a serious risk of catching cold. Your symptoms certainly sound grave, but I can't possibly make a firm diagnosis till you've been to the radiologist.' I held up a test-tube to the light and shook my head: 'Alas, the old familiar *faeces*. There's some radical endocrine imbalance – perhaps more serious than you think yourself!'

He went away chuckling. Not at my little joke, which he didn't see; but because he was convinced he had got the better of me.

As soon as he was out of the door, I hung my stethoscope round my neck and sat down quickly at my desk. By the time the Chief-Inspector was ushered in, I was absorbed in writing up the valetudinarian's case-card. I was the very picture, or so I hoped, of the dedicated general practitioner.

'What can I do for you, Inspector?'

As we shook hands I felt my prepared expression stiffen with the shock of recognition. There could be no doubt about that square red face; about the tow-coloured hair now haloed by the martyrdom of a tight bowler; about that swelling, paramilitary thorax that seemed sewn rather than buttoned into the tight blue overcoat. It was 'Blanco' Buxton, the worst of the House Monitors during my first year at Charterhouse. A stickler for discipline and the absurd privileges of the bloods, he had shone mainly in the O.T.C. and the very sight of him brought back bitter memories of afternoons wasted in the changing-room, blancoing, brassoing and kiwiing his Under Officer's equipment.

But his grey, slightly hyperthyroid eyes revealed no flicker of recognition, and that gave me initial self-confidence.

'Sorry to cut in like this,' he said. 'Your man refused to let me wait my turn. . . . Got a guilty conscience probably. . . . Extraordinary how many people have!'

I smiled grimly. 'Won't you take off your coat and hat and sit down?'

He folded his coat and placed it on the examination couch with his bowler hat on top. He hitched up his well-creased trousers and sat down beside the neat pile.

'I see you've got a midday paper on your desk. You've probably guessed why I've come to see you?'

I nodded.

'Nasty business altogether. You knew the old girl, didn't you? Lady Killaloe tells me you're an old friend of the family as well as being the family doctor?'

I nodded and waited patiently.

'Incidentally, can you tell me – without betraying any professional secrets, of course – just what is the matter with that attractive young woman? When I saw her this morning I had the impression either that she was doped or was being evasive. . . .'

'*Evasive?*' – I did my best to look amused at the suggestion. – 'She's extremely absent-minded, if that's what you mean. But she also happens to be an asthmatic, and last night she had two quarter grains of ephedrine. She didn't get to bed till very late, as you know, and it's possible she didn't sleep straight away – ephedrine has that effect. With only four hours' sleep, and on top of that a frightful shock, I doubt if even you would have been able to answer questions coherently!'

'No, I suppose not.' He was staring at me oddly, fingering his stubbly rectangular moustache, while my uncle's pyramid clock on the mantelpiece ticked away like a death-watch beetle.

'You seem to have hit your forehead, doctor?'

'Yes, I hit it on an ashtray in a car.' As I said this my forehead began to pulse gently, and I felt sure that the abrasion had gone red.

'Now about this party you had here last night,' he was saying: 'Could anybody else have known about it?'

'It wasn't a party exactly. It was just my wife and I and Lady Killaloe and her ... her friend, Mr McBane. I don't think anybody could have known about it – unless of course they told somebody.'

'For instance,' – he seemed dissatisfied with my answer – 'when did you make the arrangement?'

'On Wednesday night, when Lady Killaloe was driving us home from a night-club.'

He was writing now in a black notebook: 'Ah, which night club? . . . Thank you . . . Was Lady Killaloe with Mr McBane?'

'She was with another friend, Mr Paul Latta.'

'Two Ts? . . . Good . . . Did you make the arrangement for last night in his presence?'

'No . . . No, I'm sure we didn't.'

'And last night, when Lady Killaloe and Mr McBane were here – were there any telephone calls? Any social calls, I mean? . . . None whatever . . . I see. *And what time did your guests leave you?*'

He was staring at me again with his dull but definitely radioactive eyes, his pencil sticking from the corner of his mouth.

I hesitated. The pulse in my forehead hammered at my brain. I was struggling with an impulse to tell the truth and let Pat get out of it as best she could. Suddenly he said: 'You know, doctor, I'm certain I've seen you before somewhere.'

The unexpected stay of execution provoked another fit of nervous levity. 'Perhaps it was at Bow Street,' I improvised.

'In my student days I was once wrongly arrested and charged with setting fire to a telephone kiosk!'

'Your *student* days, eh?' Now he was reaching for his pipe, visibly relaxing into a more genial mood. From another pocket he produced a silk tobacco pouch striped with the Old Carthusian colours. . . .

'Now I've got you taped! You were at Gownboys, that young Mortimer who couldn't keep quiet during prep. – am I right?' He let the tobacco pouch unfurl like a banner, daring me to deny the old school colours.

'All right,' I said, 'all right, I'll come quietly. You must be Blanco Buxton, the Hammer of the House, the Fury of the Fags! God, how it all comes back!'

He chuckled complacently, waggling his finger at me. 'I bet you were as bad when you became a Monitor yourself. You had quite a career as a racquets player and no doubt you wielded a pretty useful stick when it came to enforcing discipline. Well, well, this is quite an occasion. You'll hardly credit it, Mortimer, but you're the first Carthusian I've spoken to for three years. You see, most of my colleagues in the Force have a different background . . . excellent fellows, of course, but . . . ' he broke off, puffing his pipe to hide his embarrassment . . . 'but I'm wasting your time. Now, let's see, where were we? . . . Oh yes, can you confirm Lady Killaloe's statement that she and Mr McBane left your house at four o'clock this morning?'

'I certainly can. I was so exhausted by that time that I kept glancing at the clock, hoping they would take the hint. I . . .'

'Good. Lady K. must have been more on the spot than I thought. . . . Excuse me, you were going to add something else?'

I felt bolder now. The lie seemed to have gone down whole, and his manner had become very friendly. 'I was wondering,' I said, 'why you asked that question? It occurred to me I might be more use to you if I knew what you were trying to get at.'

'Why, of course, old boy. I was only trying to save your time. As you know yourself, if you read detective stories, one of the first things we do in this sort of investigation is to establish the time-limits within which the crime could have been committed. Now Lady K. tells me that after leaving you she drove McBane to his hotel in Cromwell Road and then went straight home, parking the car in front of the house. In other words, the crime must have been committed by quarter past four.'

I concealed my relief by scratching my head stupidly. 'You mean, after that time the thief wouldn't have risked it?'

'Exactly. He knew the car, he knew the house, and he knew the habits of the occupants. He knew Mrs Tatham was away for the weekend, *and he had every reason to believe that Annie Bligh was away for the night.*'

He let this sink in for a moment, then continued: 'As you probably know, Annie Bligh has an unmarried sister in Ealing, to whom she went every Friday as regular as clockwork to spend the night. Last night everything went as usual. After a good tuck-in the two old girls planned to go to the last house at the Carlton in Ealing Broadway. They were standing outside Ealing station, waiting for a bus, when Annie suddenly decided to return to London immediately – she thought she had forgotten to switch off the electric iron in the kitchen. Her train went at nine-thirty, so she must have been home by about half-past ten.'

Buxton paused and puffed furiously at his pipe, just in time to save a thin wisp of smoke from withering into the ashy bowl.

'And that gives you the other time-limit?'

'No, we can get closer than that, a lot closer. When she got home she had a cup of tea, filled her hot-water bottle and went up to bed. Her room, incidentally, is on the top floor, where all the servants sleep. But she didn't go to sleep at once. On the carpet by her bed was a letter from a brother in New Zealand, which her sister had given her to take home and read at leisure. It looks as if she dozed off and was awakened later by a suspicious noise. I found her window fully opened from the bottom, though she normally had only a crack of air at the top; which suggests that, just as she was putting on her dressing-gown to go down and investigate the suspicious noise, she heard a car draw up at the pavement and looked out to see if it was Lady Killaloe coming home . . . '

'Stop a minute,' I interrupted, 'is that guesswork about the car?'

'Certainly not. My theory is that the noise she heard was a heavy tread in the room below, which is Mrs Tatham's bedroom. The man believed, remember, that he was alone in the house, and it must have given him a nasty shock to hear Annie moving over his head. He had no time to get Lady Killaloe's jewellery, which, though much less valuable than Mrs Tatham's, was in fact far more accessible. He ran downstairs to the basement, intending to leave by the area door. But just as he reached it he heard a car draw up, and thought, like Annie Bligh, that it was Lady Killaloe's. In fact, it was the neighbour's debutante daughter being brought home by her escort. It was a quarter to three, and the two young people stood talking for a good quarter of an hour, leaning against the railings of Mrs Tatham's area. While they were there, the man who was listening at the area door heard footsteps on the stairs behind him. He nipped back along the passage and hid in the recess under the basement stairs, hoping that Annie Bligh – he must have realized by then who it was – would go past him into the kitchen. Then, I imagine, the passage light went on, including the one specially placed to light up the gloryhole where he was hiding. That light must have put him in a panic. But it also enabled him to see a short length of lead piping, now missing, left behind by a plumber who had been working on the kitchen sink. He knew he was cornered, you see, completely cornered. But the savage way he set about her seems to me quite unmotivated unless he knew that her survival would mean his being identified. *In other words, she must have seen him, face to face . . .*'

He broke off and, striding over to the window, knocked out his pipe on the window-sill. His face, as he turned, was glowing with professional self-satisfaction. 'Any flaws so far, Doctor?'

I said, 'There's only one thing that strikes me as implausible. If he really believed that Annie was away for the night, why didn't he come earlier? Surely Lady Killaloe might have been expected home any time after eleven?'

'Ah, I was hoping you would ask me that one. I found the explanation on the drawing-room mantelpiece at Ovington Square – an invitation to the opening of a bottle-club called the Chinchilla, one of those joints that don't start up till the other night clubs are closing down. How was the thief to know she had decided to spend the evening with you when she had written across the top of the printed card "Pick up Paul from Ciro's after one"? I suppose that would be Mr Latta again?'

I shrugged my shoulders: 'Ask her – you're working on the certainty that the man was in touch with one of the servants?'

He nodded grimly. 'Mrs Tatham gets back tonight. Tomorrow morning, or perhaps even tonight, I shall parade the whole bunch for inspection. Meanwhile I'm interested in getting to know more about a girl called Mollie Rideout – a lady's-maid Mrs Tatham sacked because she caught her wearing the jade earrings she had given Lady Killaloe for Christmas. I suppose you can't help me there?'

'I know nothing against the girl, if that's what you mean. Lady Killaloe *gave* her the earrings, which was generous if not very tactful. And of course, when Mrs Tatham sacked her, Lady Killaloe felt very responsible. I believe she set her up in a small dressmaking business and sent her rich friends along.'

'Well, thank you.' Buxton had got to his feet and was standing in front of my desk with his legs wide apart, absorbed by the study of his pointed black shoes. 'You've been most cooperative, Doctor. Though I wouldn't have expected any less from a fellow Carthusian. . . . ' He thrust his hands deep in his pockets and rocked gently on his feet like a great square mechanical puppet with a lump of lead shifting inside him.

Eventually he looked up and said: 'By the way – I happened to notice a letter on the hall table, addressed to the secretary of the Wildman Club. You'll forgive my policeman's curiosity, but are you by any chance a member?'

'I am. But that letter contains my resignation. As a married man, I don't seem to have much use for a club nowadays, and the subscription keeps going up. . . . '

'Ah, I see. Charming club though, nice atmosphere. I just wondered if you knew my chief, Sir Roy Anstruther?'

'Well, I've drunk with him and lunched at the same table. But he's rather a big pot for me. One might as well have lunched with the Home Secretary, if you see what I mean. Remote, no real contact.'

'You found that? Well, I suppose I've a bit more contact, being in the same racket as it were. Matter of fact I was lunching with him myself the other day and I was very struck with the place. Good grub too, and we had a bottle of Château something-or-other that you can't get anywhere else. The chief told me I ought to have a club, and though I laughed and said "Coppers don't belong to clubs!" I did give the matter a bit of thought. It occurred to me I might do worse than this Wildman Club. But I didn't dare ask the Chief to put me up for it in case he thought I was sticking out my neck. That's why I wondered if you, as a fellow Carthusian . . .'

I thought for a second. Then I said, 'Of course I'll be very glad to put you up. But I'll have to prepare the ground a bit. Look, why don't you come and lunch with me there one day next week – say Wednesday?'

I owed it to Pat and ourselves to foster his ambitions. And he seemed quite delighted with me.

As we shook hands I was thinking: *In other words she must have seen him face to face. . . .*

Chapter 4

Siren on the Rocks

'I KNEW he was a detective,' Sally said, 'because he wouldn't let Llewellyn take his hat and coat. I was leaning over the banisters when he went and I felt like spitting on his head . . . what's the matter? Did you have to lie about last night?'

'I did. And he's not the sort of man one enjoys lying to. But when he found out we were at school together, he started eating out of my hand. No, there's absolutely nothing to worry about, provided nobody saw Pat's car outside Cynthia Andrei's flat . . . I would feel safer if I knew about that. Could you go round and see Pat?'

Where romance is concerned, women are born conspirators, and Sally was visibly uplifted by this development. 'Is it really urgent? Okay, I'll go at once.'

Then a thought struck her and she said, 'No, you go. If there are reporters or detectives prowling about the house, a professional visit would arouse less interest than a social one.'

'It *is* urgent, and I've got appointments till five. Besides, I think Pat would rather see *you* just now.'

She agreed to go, only to ring me five minutes later on the house telephone. 'I've been thinking it over, and *from every point of view* I'm sure it would be better if you went.'

I knew too much about Sally's mental processes to argue.

It was lighting-up time when I got to Ovington Square. The lamps, contending with pallid sunset sinking into the trees and shrubs of the garden, had a decorative, theatrical look. I hurried on stage past the policeman and the group of onlookers, up the steps of Number Ten.

'That's the 'Ome Office doctor,' said a woman's voice as I stood waiting for the door to open. 'You can tell by 'is black bag.'

'Don't be weedy, Liz,' said a male voice. 'They took the body away this morning. That must be *'er* doctor; they say she's ill from nervous shock.'

'Serves 'er right too, if you ask me. Wouldn't ever 'ave 'appened if she'd got 'ome at a respectable hour.'

I was about to give up ringing the bell and turn tail when the door was opened by Pat herself. She was wearing a nylon dressing-gown over practically nothing and she looked dishevelled as well as exhausted. Her public must have enjoyed this personal appearance in the powerful light of the porch.

'It's a good thing you came,' she said, banging the door. 'Dugald's just gone to Victoria to fetch Mummy and the staff, and we're in for a pretty grim evening. Come up and talk to me while I'm dressing.'

Her room was in chaos. There was a tray on the floor beside the disordered bed; clothes were strewn about on the chairs; an ashtray overflowed on to the glass-topped dressing-table, already pink with spilt face-powder.

'How are you feeling?' I asked, removing her brassière from an armchair and sitting down.

'I've been trying to catch up on sleep – ' she unrolled a silk stocking up one of her long shapely legs – 'actually I'm feeling lousy.'

My eye fell on a little bottle of sleeping tablets. The cap was off and it had fallen over, dribbling a string of green beads among the jars of face-cream on the bedside table. 'How many of those did you take last night? I've just had a visit from Buxton and he wanted to know why you were so dopey this morning.'

'Buxton? . . . oh, the Inspector. Well, I hope you told him it was none of his damned business. Actually I only had two.

What with the ephedrine and the excitement, I couldn't sleep at the flat. That's why I came back here.' She picked up her brassière from the back of my chair and disappeared into the bathroom.

I said: 'I should have thought you would have slept naturally – in the circumstances.'

'One can't have everything.'

I considered the implications of this cryptic remark while water swished and Pat scrubbed her teeth. She hadn't bothered to close the bathroom door, and I felt ill-at-ease, unprofessional, in the intimacy of this relationship at this particular moment. I felt I had to get on with what I had come to say, instead of sitting there uneasily enjoying the privilege.

'His bark was worse than his bite? That's what I thought too.'

'I didn't say that. I said *he asked about last night*. This is important. I'll wait till you've turned off that water. I don't want to shout.'

She emerged a moment later in pants and brassière, apparently unaware that she was underdressed. Her body was beautifully firm and slim. The only defect, a slight over-expansion of the thoracic cage, with a corresponding heightening of the shoulders, only made her breasts more provocative.

She bent down and took a cigarette from the packet on my knee and waited till I lit it for her.

'What did he ask about last night?'

'He asked what time you and Dugald left . . . Don't look so worried – it must have been all over by then, you see.'

She sat down on the bed and stared at me vaguely: 'You mean, if I'd come home earlier he might not have tried it?'

'He would have seen the car parked outside the house. But he was as certain about your not coming home before three as he was about the absence of Annie and your foster-mother. He, or his inside contact, had seen the invitation to the opening of the Chinchilla Club on which you had thoughtfully scribbled down your date with Paul. When did you cancel that?'

'The same evening. I rang up and told him I was too tired to go out.'

'How did he take it?'

'Oh, he didn't mind a bit.'

'And when he learns from the papers that you didn't get in till four, what will his reactions be?'

'Calm, I imagine. He's used to my excuses. Who could have known about that invitation, I wonder?'

'I'm coming to that. First, I want to make sure about the alibi. I forgot to ask you this morning: could anybody have seen you going to Cynthia Andrei's flat?'

She thought for a moment, then shook her head: 'Uh-huh. I left the car in Devonshire Street. And nobody in the Mews would think twice about goings-on in Cynthia's flat. She distributes her latchkeys like largesse.'

'Then I think we can forget about it. Or, better still, think ourselves into the lie until we really believe it. That should be easy for you!'

Pat was wriggling into a tight black dress and presently she emerged, panting. She combed back her hair with her fingers and stood for a moment with her palms covering her temples, as though struck by a sudden thought.

'It's not so easy for me to believe my own lies when Mummy has to be convinced too.'

'What's wrong with this one from her point of view?'

'You're being dense, David. Don't you remember when she checked on that alibi for Dickie and found you weren't in London that weekend?'

'But that was years ago. I'm accepted now, respectable.'

'That's why she won't believe we stayed so late at your house. She thinks my nightlife is one long orgy. . . . Will you do me up, please? I always get my flesh caught in this zip.'

I zipped the fastening carefully and said to her back:

'So she won't be disappointed if she *does* see through the alibi. With an appalling crime just committed in her house, she's not going to gripe about your sexual peccadilloes. Doesn't she approve of Dugald?'

'My dear, she dotes on him. She treats him as a sort of wild pet. He's even allowed to bite her hand occasionally. I think she's a bit in love with him really. She wants me to marry him because she thinks he's good for me. Yet because I'm not her real daughter she's also jealous. . . . ' She flung herself down on the bed moodily, only to jump up a moment later at the sound of voices from below. 'There they are. . . . Go down and meet them, will you? I must do something about my awful face. . . . '

As I reached the landing Mrs Tatham's voice was shrilling through the house like a burglar alarm approximately sixteen hours too late. I felt as though the whole ugly business were only now about to begin.

The stairs straightened out to reveal the group standing in the hall. All were dressed in black except Dugald: all talked softly except Mrs Tatham. The light from the chandelier flashed back from her diamond brooch as she turned and put her hand on Dugald's arm.

'I insist on your staying to supper,' she was saying. – 'No, of course we don't want to be alone.'

Now she and Dugald were standing apart, leaving Cumberledge, the butler, smoothing his bowler hat; while Mrs Cumberledge and the housemaid stood holding their suitcases waiting for orders.

'You can manage something cold, can't you, Mrs Cumberledge? . . . Good, that's all then . . . No, wait a minute.

My daughter's probably forgotten to keep the kitchen fire in, and if you *can* manage to get the water hot in time, I'd very much like a bath tonight. . . . Yes, that's all, Mrs Cumberledge . . . What? . . . Oh well, Cumberledge will go with you, if you're *both* frightened.' Flash: 'I suppose it's *all right* down in the basement, Dugald?'

The servants, with Cumberledge in the lead, were tiptoeing towards the kitchen stairs offstage, when – flash! 'Oh, Cumberledge? Will you tell that policeman outside the door to send those morbid sightseers away . . .'

'Well,' she said, when the servants had disappeared, 'I must say I expected Pat to be *here* to greet us – since she didn't feel strong enough to come to the station. . . . Who's that coming down the stairs . . . Ah, David! I thought for a moment it was somebody else, a detective or one of those snoopers from the newspapers. Does Pat know I've arrived?'

'She'll be down in a minute. But I must warn you that she's not in very good shape, as is only too natural. If I were you I wouldn't be in too great a hurry to put her through last night's horrors all over again. The effect of remembering and describing what Nature is trying to put out of her mind, so as to enable her to get over the nervous shock, should be avoided as far as is humanly possible.'

This prolix speech kindled a light in Dugald's eye that I took for admiration. But Mrs Tatham wasn't impressed.

'What rubbish, David! The best way to get horrors out of your mind is to talk about them. And, anyway, who said I was going to "put her through it"? All I was saying to Dugald when you appeared, was that she should have been here to meet me. Both of you are so concerned about Pat that you've no time to consider the shock I've suffered – and at my age too. There she is!'

Pat was treading downstairs delicately, watching her green slippers from step to step, as though afraid of falling. Her face looked quite ashy with powder and her lips pouted a shade of rouge that clashed abominably with her hair.

'I'm sorry I couldn't come and meet you, Mummy. David thinks I may have strained my heart wheezing.'

'Yes,' I said, 'I didn't want to give you any more worry just now. But the fact is, she has a slight grumble. No quarrels, please. No emotional stress.' I looked hard at Dugald and winked.

'And late nights?' Mrs Tatham had intercepted my message. 'Were you thinking of her heart, David, when you kept her up drinking and smoking till four this morning?'

Dugald's eyebrows arched slightly: 'Come now, Mrs Tatham. There's been murder done in this house, and it's no earthly use bellyaching about late nights like a one-man Kirk Session about a breach of the Sabbath Day observance.'

Mrs Tatham's reaction was no less astonishing.

'Dugald,' she said severely, 'no one has ever dared to speak to me as you do; not even my husband, who was Master of the Quorn and habitually treated people like dogs. You're a rough diamond, but at least you're not decadent like Pat's other men. Now let's go into the drawing-room and get a drink.'

Chapter 5

Me and My Shadow

MRS TATHAM had been a beauty. She was sixty now and frighteningly well preserved. Flesh and blood seemed to have crystallized in the process. With her silver-washed curls and the mask of make-up, neither joy nor grief suited her. But Pat's cold, almost laconic account of how she had found Annie that morning seemed to call for display of proper feeling. Mrs Tatham dabbed at her eyes with a handkerchief.

In fact Mrs Tatham's feelings for Nanny had been far from warm, ever since Nanny had refused to admit that Pat's character was due to bad heredity. Nanny had even hinted that it was all Mrs Tatham's fault, for adopting the prettiest little girl she could find in the orphanage of which she was patroness, then treating the child as a personal adornment. Still, Nanny was dead and it wasn't pleasant to have to recall how often she had threatened Pat: 'Nanny's getting above herself again: this time I shall have to get rid of her.' The easiest way of forgetting that was to accuse Pat of being callous.

'I simply can't understand you, Pat. You always pretended to be so fond of her. Yet when she was lying in the mortuary, murdered, it never occurred to you to send any flowers. Just for Nellie Bligh's sake that would have been decent.'

Pat rose, expressionless, and went to pour herself another drink: 'Not long ago you were accusing Nanny of having "alienated my affections". I'm not going to feel guilty for you, Mummy. You know quite well how I felt and feel.'

'Guilty! How *dare* you talk like that? It was time for Nanny to retire and have a little life of her own.'

'The time for that was when I first got married. You kept her on because she was a marvellous housekeeper and because you didn't want to have to pension her off.'

'All right, then' – Mrs Tatham sank back on her cushion with a sigh of exhaustion – 'I shall try and be as hard as you are. There's one thing that puzzles me very much about poor Nanny's behaviour last night. She was, as you say, wonderfully trustworthy and I feel bound to say it was most unlike her to go out like that leaving the house completely empty.'

'But it was Friday night – her night out.' Pat sat up suddenly. She had been nursing her whisky and some of it spilt down her dress. 'You know she always goes to Nellie on Fridays; wet or fine, summer or winter.'

'But this Friday was different. I had specially asked her not to go out unless she knew you were going to be in. There's been so much in the papers lately about weekend burglaries.'

Pat's mouth fell open and she clasped her hands on her chest, staring at Mrs Tatham blankly: 'God, it's just occurred to me – what if I promised to stay in and forgot all about it? ... I couldn't ever forgive myself....'

'Then perhaps you didn't, dear.' Mrs Tatham's irony was triumphantly dental. 'Perhaps Nanny misunderstood you?'

Dugald said sternly: 'I don't see how she could have promised that, knowing we were going round to David's. In any case the point seems relatively trivial.'

Before Mrs Tatham could rally I weighed in heavily: 'Trivial actions sometimes have serious results. But there's no question here of cause and effect, or Annie would be responsible for her own death by forgetting to turn off the iron. ... Incidentally, I'm the only one here who knows the lines the police are working on. I had a visit three hours ago from the Chief Inspector in charge of the case....'

When I had finished describing the interview – I carefully said nothing about Mollie Rideout so as not to start Pat and Mrs Tatham quarrelling again – they were all silent for a moment, impressed. Then Dugald said: 'Scotland Yard haven't lost much time, have they? And from what I've heard they're as thorough as mechanical dredgers. They bring up all the dirt first, and then experts go through it with microscopes.' He looked meaningly from Pat to me. 'Did he by any chance tell you if he suspected anybody in particular?'

'He made it plain that the crime couldn't have been committed without the collaboration of somebody in the house. I'm afraid the servants are in for a grilling.'

'Ridiculous, absolutely ridiculous,' said Mrs Tatham. 'Cumberledge and his wife are beyond suspicion. And Johnson has been with me twenty years. I shall not allow them to be suspected. Why, they'll probably leave me if they think I can't protect them from this outrage. If the Inspector has no better suspect, I have: and I shan't hesitate to tell him. I can explain why only *my* jewels were taken . . .'

'*Who* do you suspect?' There was a crouching tension in Pat's voice.

'Mollie Rideout, of course. She's a bad lot, and she's always hated me for giving her what she deserved.'

'Of all the mean things! . . .' Pat began, and I said: 'Keep your wool on, Pat. If they don't know already from Nellie Bligh, they're bound to find out about her from the servants.'

'Of course they will,' Mrs Tatham said. 'They'll find out that she's been coming to this house to give Pat fittings. They'll find out about that delinquent brother of hers who was always hanging about round the kitchen. . . . They'll connect this crime with the jewel robbery at Edna de Hartung's in Mount Street. You, Pat, were so anxious for Mollie to succeed in dressmaking that you even sent *my* friends to her – again, of course, behind my back . . . Well, Cumber-ledge, what is it?'

Cumberledge, who had been trying to strike a balance between discreet coughings and a pharyngeal paroxysm, advanced into the room as if he had heard nothing. 'Telephone for Doctor Mortimer.' He might have been announcing the death of my next-of-kin.

When I returned a few minutes later Dugald was saying: 'On the face of it, I'd say she was completely innocent. She would have known she was bound to be suspected. . . . '

I said, 'I'm sorry, I've got to go. I've got a premature labour in Sloane Street.'

Dugald came to the door, looking embarrassed. He gripped my hand with both his: 'David, I'd like to thank you for all you're doing for Pat, and, incidentally, for me.'

I didn't realize how much I was doing, or I shouldn't have murmured: 'Oh forget it. Anything to stop Fate messing up people's lives.'

My 'premature labour' was Nellie Bligh. 'She's in the waiting-room,' Sally told me. 'But she absolutely refuses to tell me what she wants.'

Nellie was a gaunt, elderly woman with a tiresomely confidential manner. Anything she had to say about people was invariably said in a low voice with significant nodding and eyebrow-raising. She didn't want to be thought a gossip, though *in her position she couldn't help hearing confidential things, etc.*

'Doctor Mortimer!' she said, tragically, rising from a pile of *Queens* on the oak dining-table, 'I *had* to come and see you. My poor sister used to say you were such a fine man. She said if anything ever went wrong in the family she would rather go to you than Mrs Tatham.'

'Sit down and tell me all about it. You know how fond I always was of Annie.'

'Oh I know, I know, Doctor Mortimer. I know you wouldn't ever believe that my sister *betrayed her trust*.'

'Betrayed her trust?'

'Last night – she didn't really *want* to come to Ealing. Mrs Tatham was worried about the house, you see. But Pat – I can't get used to her fancy name – Pat *insisted* on her coming and *promised to stay in all night*. My sister loved her as if she were her own child, you know, and however many lies she told Mrs Tatham, she never believed Pat would lie to her....' A few dry sobs broke from Nellie, and she stared at me nervously, twisting her gloves in her lap. '*If she'd kept that promise my sister might be alive now....*'

I stared at her for a moment. Then I asked: 'Did you tell the police about that?'

'Oh no, Doctor Mortimer. I'm not one of those to make trouble. But I thought I'd come and tell *you*, because it's not nice keeping things to oneself with the police asking so many questions.'

'No, it isn't nice at all.... Look, Miss Bligh, shall we keep this knowledge to ourselves?'

She didn't answer at once and I didn't like the expression on her face. I added: 'For your sister's sake. I don't think she would have wanted Mrs Tatham to know, do you?'

She hesitated, twisting her gloves. Then suddenly she came out with it.

'I'm not so sure. You see, Annie was going to have retired soon with a nice little pension for her old age which should have helped both of us to make ends meet. Now Annie's gone I suppose I've no right to expect anything from *Mrs Tatham*, particularly if she thinks *Annie betrayed her trust*....'

'Ah, I see, yes, that's a very good point, very reasonable indeed. I'll tell you what we'll do. If you'll agree to keep this a secret with me for the present, I'll have a talk with Pat and put it to her that she at any rate has a moral obligation to see you're all right financially, and I'm certain she would rather tell the truth, however awkward for her, than let her mother think anything against Annie.'

She got up and wrung my hand gratefully. 'You mustn't think I mind about the money. I just couldn't bear the thought of any *shadow* resting on my dear sister's memory after she served them so faithfully all those years.'

Sally called me into the kitchen where she was already cooking the dinner. Saturday, Llewellyn's night out, was our great opportunity for staying in, and was usually celebrated by a dinner in the framework of Sally's Foreign Cooking series.

'What's on the menu tonight?' I asked suspiciously, opening the oven door and sniffing. 'It smells like the Casbah.'

'Wrong by about three hundred miles. It's a *mouton à la provençale* garnished with onions, peppers and aubergines. . . . Now what about Miss Bligh?'

She listened intently, squatting on her haunches before the oven and basting the mutton with a salad spoon.

'I'd always heard she was a poisonous old creature!' She got up and removed the cigarette dangling from the corner of her mouth. 'To start grabbing so soon! – the very day after her sister's murder – and in this blackmailing way!'

'She's old and poor, and she probably associates Annie with the comforts her wages brought. No, that doesn't shock me as much as Pat's behaviour. To send Annie out against her will and then go out herself seems to me pointless irresponsibility . . . unless . . . '

'Unless what?' Sally was rubbing her right eye with her fist and the left eye looked at me penetratingly. 'What on earth are you suggesting?'

'Oh nothing. I just wish Pat weren't such a liar. It complicates things.'

'Why are you suddenly so against Pat? After all, it was Nanny's night out. So why keep her back just because Mrs Tatham was worried about her rotten old sparklers? In Pat's shoes I would probably have done just the same. Don't you know that feeling one has about fussy people? One wants to prove that they are fussing about nothing?'

I said: 'Why are you suddenly so pro-Pat?'

She brought out the mutton, sizzling and iridescent, and I set about it irritably with the carving knife, wondering how long we were going to continue hiding from each other behind false attitudes.

'Did you have to put in quite so much garlic?' I asked, chewing a *gousse* she had artfully embedded in the well-done bit at the end of the joint.

'The recipe's from *Peasant Cooking in Provence*, and actually the joint should be stuck all over with bits of garlic. But if you're so frightfully HAH-ley Street, you don't have to eat it.'

Sally thought me philistine. She knew I really preferred fishing to monumentalizing in Roman Provence and she was always trying to educate me.

I opened my mouth and breathed HAH-ley back at her. 'I've got it,' I said, snapping my fingers. 'I've solved a major mystery of the ancient world.'

'Of what set fire to the Library at Alexandria? Or why they all abandoned Knossos?'

'Of why Nebuchadnezzar ate chlorophyll. He wasn't mad at all. He had a concubine called Nenuphar who didn't like the way his breath smelt.'

Sally murmured something about grass-widows, then abruptly she dropped the ball: 'Darling, we're talking like strangers at a cocktail party when the eye is fixed on somebody beyond. Don't you think, to coin a phrase, that we ought to return to our muttons – before Llewellyn sneaks back from the pub and we have to start talking in whispers?'

An hour later we were still discussing the crime. Sally had been speculating about the murderer, and now, inevitably, she was putting herself in the position of his woman. 'I would know, I'm certain I would know. But if I really loved him it wouldn't make any difference. If anything –' she stared at me till I felt I had blood on my hands – 'If anything I would love him more . . . Christmas! Do you hear what I hear?' She shivered, and the smoke of her cigarette suddenly changed direction.

'Yes,' I said, 'yes, I certainly do . . . '

For a moment we both listened to the voice. It was a beery baritone, comic in itself, but made slightly eerie by the tremolo and the jaunty old-time music-hall style.

> '*Me and my shadow*
> *Walkin' down the avenoo-a.*'

The front door banged and he started again, this time opening up *fortissimo*. No doubt he wanted to test the acoustic properties of the hall. But I think he was also trying to exorcise its gloom before sinking back to sobriety from the relative gaiety of Saturday night at the Local.

ME! He hit the high note at the beginning of the next line, liked the sound of it, and repeated ME-ME-ME-ME.

Silence was momentarily re-established, to be broken by a dull thud and the archaic booming of our dinner gong, a museum piece since my uncle's time.

'Go on, darling,' said Sally. 'This is a man's job!'

When I switched on the hall light Llewellyn was still sitting where he had landed, against the staircase, after sliding across the floor on a Persian rug. The extraordinary part of it was that he had somehow managed to get his legs through the gong-stand without upsetting it. And now, with his Homburg hat on the back of his head, he was sitting there on the floor, dazed and resentful in the sudden light, like a felon in the stocks who has the sun in his eyes and can't see who has flung the rotten egg.

'Ohboyohboy,' he groaned. 'Whataloadobeer, whata-fugginloadobeer.'

'Llewellyn,' I said sternly, 'you're drunk. You're disgustingly drunk.'

Sober, he had the mask of a death's-head. Drunk, he looked much more human; there was a candle in that Hallow'een pumpkin, and the hollows were less cavernous. He blinked, then staggered to his feet, swaying; but sobered by the shock.

' 'Scush me, sir. I seem to have forgot myself.'

'We'll talk about that tomorrow,' I said. 'Now off you go to bed and sleep it off.'

He stared at me for a moment, then shook his head slowly, staggered a few steps towards the kitchen and sank down on the bottom stair with his hand to his head.

'It's my head, sir. I've got my headaches back again like I used to have them after the patient coshed me with the bottle. I wanted to go and get a skinful, but there was too much of a crowd at the bar and I couldn't get served quick enough.'

'Headaches? You haven't had them for years. And what's this about not getting served quick enough? You seem to have got your skinful all right.'

He frowned, trying to straighten things out in his mind. 'That was lash night – I couldn't sleep, shee, and you and Mrs Mortimer had company . . . that's ri', you had company, and by the time they was gone it was midni' . . . that's ri', it was midnight because I heard the 'all clock strike . . . I didn't like to come up for a tablet . . . '

I was no longer laughing inwardly. I was cold, icy cold.

'That's not true, Llewellyn. It was four in the morning when my guests left. And you were asleep – do you hear me? Fast asleep. Otherwise you would have taken some codeine from the dispensary and told me about it in the morning. Now who put you up to this? Who have you been talking to?'

'Nobody,' he said sullenly. He looked down and started rubbing his hands.

'Who was it, Llewellyn?' For the first time I almost liked him for his stupidity; it became nakeder as he sobered out of his artificial self-confidence.

'Nobody,' he repeated. 'You're just finding a 'scush to sack me. All ri', go on sack me and see what happens! . . . Ohboyohboywhataloadobeer.'

I said, 'Now listen carefully, if you can. This is the first time you've been drunk so as to worry me, and I'm perfectly prepared to overlook it, especially as you've obviously been filled up by somebody deliberately trying to make you drunk. But I can't do anything for you if you tell me lies. If by tomorrow you can't remember the truth, you'd better pack your bags and be gone, before I get on to Scotland Yard. Now go and sleep on that.'

He staggered off whispering to himself 'Ohboyohboy.'

Sally's arm slid through mine as I stood there watching him go. 'David, you should have got it out of him while he was still drunk and confused.'

I said: 'Give him time to sleep and then to brood in his crapula. What he really fears is change. He was fifteen years in that asylum and twenty years with my uncle, and he would rather die than live away from doctors, away from headache pills and the little scraps of medical knowledge which justify his existence in his own estimation.'

Chapter 6

A Look of Cunning

THAT night, for the first time for months, I was aware of the rush and rumble of traffic along Sloane Street and Knightsbridge. Even our backwater seemed to throb with the pulse of the main arteries. The red lining of our curtains glowed and flickered, and taxi-meters tinkled like cash registers as drivers dumped their fares and whined away again, rushing their ascending scales of speed. Once, towards morning, the fire-engines from Basil Street went clanging southwards to doctor some outbreak that inflamed the low London sky. But the flickering electricity of worry, actuating the cells of the sleepless brain, could not be calmed so easily.

Who had been getting at Llewellyn? Scotland Yard? A detective from the Insurance Company? A 'private eye' hired by Killaloe?

Was he merely trying to check the alibi? Or had he some reason to believe it was false?

It was Sally who eventually voiced the most unpleasant thought of all – the thought I had been trying to push down into the sump of my consciousness.

'Has it occurred to you that somebody might be planning to blackmail you; or Pat, or both? Surely a detective wouldn't have approached Llewellyn like that?'

'They do that sort of thing in novels.'

'Well, they might conceivably fill him up with beer to make him talk. But why should they put ideas in his head?'

I thought about this while Sally got up to get a drink of water: we had decided to take sleeping pills. Her white nightdress, where it fell free, suddenly caught the glow of lights through the red curtains, so that her silhouette was momentarily wrapped in flame. It wasn't till later, much later, that the force of this visual impression struck me. At the moment I was thinking about Llewellyn.

Finally I said: 'I don't know. I just don't know. But if you're dealing with an intelligence like Llewellyn's, you're almost forced to put something into his head if you want to get anything out of it.'

Just as we were going to sleep Sally said: 'David, if it is a blackmailer, we're sunk. We can't let Pat down, can we?'

'No, we can't let Pat down.'

Morning brought Llewellyn to my office, where I was dealing with arrears of paperwork outstanding since our holiday in Provence. Though he was off duty, he was wearing his striped trousers and black coat; not as sackcloth and ashes, however, but as the robes of his office, the outward sign of restored self-confidence. The lapse into drunkenness, it soon emerged, had not been his fault but mine. I had called him an idiot to his face, which seemed to him untrue as well as insulting. Would my uncle – 'the finest physician in London' – have valued his services for fifteen years if he had really been an idiot?

'All right,' I said impatiently, 'all right. I called you an idiot for not realizing that Lady Killaloe needed a drink, so you went off and got drunk yourself. But that's not what I'm complaining about, and you know it. Now sit down please, and tell me what happened in the Antelope last night.'

What I got out of him, after half an hour's coarse fishing in the muddy stream of his consciousness, quite changed my attitude towards him. A Caliban of a man, but in some ways a most delicate monster. In the end I was able to congratulate him on his loyalty and honesty; to reassure him, with much personal reluctance, that his future with me was assured. . . .

'It was a woman,' I told Sally afterwards. 'Emaciated, middle-aged and shaky, wearing slacks and dirty gold sandals. She got him cornered in his favourite nook at the Antelope – you know, the one the saloon bar habitués hold sacred to "old Padded-Cells" as they call him – and by some sort of osmosis managed to get through his hide. Apparently she got him pouring out all his grievances about me – my abrupt way of speaking to him, my indifference to his headaches, how badly I compared with my uncle. When she had got him really worked up she casually picked up his evening paper. "Well in *these* circumstances" – she pointed to the headline about the murder – "I think you've been wonderfully loyal to the doctor . . . you don't see what I mean? . . . Well, apart from me, you're the only one who knows that Doctor Mortimer lied to the police to get Lady Killaloe out of an embarrassing situation. *You* know, and *I* know, that she really left the house around midnight." Llewellyn, bewildered but ready to be persuaded, protested that he hadn't heard anything. He only realized that Pat had in fact been with us by the shade of her lipstick on her glass next morning. "But you told me you hadn't slept for weeks," she said, "because of these awful headaches. So you must have heard something when they left. Anyway, you can tell Doctor Mortimer you did. And if he calls you a liar, you just give him this card and ask him to ring me up. If he admits it, your job's assured for life; you could ask for much higher pay. Whatever happens, I'll see you're all right. . . !'

I handed the card to Sally, who read out: '*Mrs Herbert Van Dopp, 30 Cathedral Street, SW1 Tel. Victoria 2350.* Do we know this old monster?'

I shook my head and she put down the pair of pants into

which she was sewing new elastic, peering at the card down a nose wrinkled with distaste.

'I don't *think* we know her. But the fact that it's a woman makes the thing even worse. . . . ' She raised the card and smelt it. 'This stinks of corruption . . . wait a moment, though. Wasn't it in Cathedral Street that Pat dropped Paul Latta the other night? Could this be the woman who keeps him?'

Pat's voice sounded small and cautious over the telephone. So I asked her if she was speaking from downstairs.

'From my bedroom actually. But if you've got anything incriminating to say, you'd better keep it till you-know-who is out of the house. He practically lives here and we've all got guilty gooseflesh by now, with the exception of my mother, of course. She initiates gooseflesh far more than Buxton does. I must say, he's been very courteous and patient, being treated like a workman in her employ. He's probably fascinated by our bad manners – as a proof that we're really high-class aristocrats.'

I said: 'I haven't anything incriminating to say. I just want to check on a new patient of mine, Mrs Van Dopp, who lives in Westminster. Could she be the elderly divorcée who poses as Paul Latta's mother?'

'She could – if she looks like a rope-ladder in an earthquake. She does? Well, you should have consulted me before taking her on. She's an evil old bitch and she hates me. I met her at Ciro's once in the aunt and she put a lighted cigarette in my pearl evening bag. Deliberately, while I was making up my face. She apologized, grinning like a gargoyle, for being so terribly short-sighted. She said she thought the bag was an ashtray. . . . '

I had hardly hung up when the telephone rang.

'Hullo? Is that Doctor Mortimer?' The voice rasped and

slipped, suggesting that her vocal cords had been screwed up too high and then frayed by hydrochloric acid. 'Van Dopp – Vera Van Dopp – you've met my son with Pat Killaloe . . . Oh, you have my *visiting card?* Well that makes everything respectable. Could you come round and see me? What? No, no, it's urgent, very urgent; I'm in agony . . .'

'What sort of agony? Where exactly?'

But the line had gone dead.

She looked as though she had slept in her clothes, the ones Llewellyn had described. She opened the door holding a cigarette in the other hand. The hand trembled so much that the ash fell right between us like a lump of fragile excrement. She peered at me with watery eyes. 'You are Doctor Mortimer, I assume? I haven't got my glasses mended yet, so I can't see you very well.'

She turned and led the way down a corridor papered with what looked like copper foil, engraved with curious submarine decorations and glowing softly to concealed lights. It was strange, passing through this restaurant-like décor, to get glimpses, through open doors, of unmade beds and scattered clothes; of a highly modern kitchen cluttered with unwashed pots and smelling strongly of garbage. The room she led me into, at the end of the passage, was long and angular like Mrs Van Dopp, with a thick white carpet, light glossy panelling, and in one corner, behind a projecting glass bookcase, a cocktail bar with chromium stools upholstered in plastic leopardskin. The only thing that struck me as significantly personal was the wealth of painted wrought iron. Every mirror and table fumed with curls and arabesques, so that there was an effect of writhing – a kind of psychotic opulence that quarrelled with the conventional boxlike chairs, with the hardness of the angles and the ruthlessness of the mirrors. And here again there was disorder and dirt – newspapers spread out on the floor, cigarette burns on the loose covers, and – oddest of all – a futuristic painting of Paul Latta's head that grew up like some monstrous white vegetable from a heavy mass of sunset and sand-dunes. This portrait hung askew, which added to the appearance of cataclysm and made one feel slightly groggy.

'You're looking at my son?' Mrs Van Dopp stopped beside me, peering. 'Everybody looks at him. He's got such a sensitive face – don't you agree? – long, like my first husband's, though without that desperate, hungry look he had. Of course I'm only his stepmother, our relationship is very free. . . .'

I said: 'Is he at home now?'

'No, he's gone to the country for the weekend . . . and just as well really' – she gave a curious delinquent chuckle – 'he wouldn't at all approve of this consultation.'

'Why wouldn't he approve?' I studied the picture of Paul, trying to imagine that smooth weak face expressing anything so formidable as disapproval.

'Because he doesn't like me seeing *doctors*. . . . Bad Vera, wicked Vera!' She waggled an already shaky finger and exposed dilapidated teeth in a slanting smile. 'But *I* like doctors. I depend on the right sort of doctor. You are the right sort, aren't you, Doctor Mortimer?'

I said: 'We'll discuss what sort of doctor I am when I know what's wrong with you. Where do you feel the pain?'

She sighed and threw herself down on the sofa with her hand resting on her stomach: 'The cramp's gone for the moment. But it'll be back again soon, worse than ever.' She raised her right knee and scratched her thigh – a long, scraping, uncivilized movement. Then, without any warning, she sneezed violently.

I said: 'All right, I understand now. You shall have it as soon as you've answered these questions. First, why do you think Lady Killaloe left my house at twelve on Friday night? And secondly, why should that detail – just supposing she and I *did* lie – have the slightest relevance to the Ovington Square murder? You must be on shaky ground, or you would have come straight to me instead of trying to suborn my manservant.'

Her face flushed dark, and for the moment I thought she was going to pick up an ashtray and fling at me. But the spasm passed, succeeded by a look of cunning.

'To answer your second question first – how should I know? It was an alibi of some sort and the police don't like alibis, whatever the motive for giving them. I know quite a lot about these things. Your first question? Well, I'll put my cards on the table. Did you know that Pat Killaloe had promised to go with Paul on Friday to the opening of the Chinchilla Club?'

'I only knew she was coming to have drinks with me.'

'Anyway, it's a fact she promised; only to ring up Paul at dinner-time with the excuse that she was too tired to go anywhere except bed. Paul's a simple boy in some ways and, though he was very disappointed, he accepted the excuse and got on to another girl. But she was going with somebody else, so about eleven he rang up Pat again to see if she wouldn't change her mind. There was no answer, which meant either that she was asleep or out. Paul reasoned to himself: "If she's gone out she must be feeling better. I'll keep on trying." Well, he kept on trying and at one o'clock Pat's number suddenly gave the engaged tone. He rang again a quarter of an hour later and it was still engaged. Ten minutes later the same result, and he realized that *Pat must have come in and gone to bed, pulling the telephone plug out of the wall . . . you see?*'

'It could equally well have been the thief who pulled the plug out of the wall.'

Again the slanting smile. 'My son has a good knowledge

of Pat's nocturnal habits and he says she always disconnects her phone before she goes to sleep; apparently she sleeps so little that when she does she wants to be sure she won't be interrupted. And why should the thief disconnect the phone? Why, pray, in a house he believed deserted? And they say the crime must have been committed at least an hour and a half later. Don't you agree that the police would be interested by this information? . . . Suppose Pat *was* at home. Suppose she was with this rather mysterious person Paul says she's in love with? . . . Wouldn't it all be rather awkward to explain? . . . '

'I don't admit your supposition for a moment. Annie Bligh might have disconnected the phone. . . . '

Paul Latta stared from his skewwise frame and the wrought iron arabesques echoed the curling smoke of our cigarettes. The *Sunday News*, stained with coffee, hung over the edge of a table, screaming KNIGHTSBRIDGE KILLER KNOWN TO VICTIM? I felt curiously degraded, inadequate.

'Has Chief Inspector Buxton been to see your son? . . . He has. Well, why did he withhold this information if he considers it so important?'

'That's just why he didn't give it. In his way he's very fond of the Killaloe girl, though she treats him abominably. He wouldn't think of betraying her.'

'What guarantee have I that he didn't in fact tell the Inspector?'

'Me, little ME!' She had a coy expression and there was a suggestion of lost beauty round the hollow cheeks, of sensuality still clinging to the pale lips. 'I need you, doctor. And if you're true to your oath, you won't deny me the means of life.'

I said: 'I'll help you temporarily, while I'm thinking things over and making enquiries. But I can't guarantee any permanent arrangement that isn't in accord with the narcotic laws and my professional conscience. Who is your usual doctor?'

'He's in trouble with the police himself. That makes you my doctor from now onwards. And I don't want any of this moralistic tripe about saving me from myself. You're not going to register me as an addict. Just give me the stuff – pure stuff, not pedlar's cut – enough at a time to save me continually running to you. You'll have to square the book as best you can. Now give me a shot – quick!'

Chapter 7

The Smooth Endocrine Flow

THE Knightsbridge bar I had chosen for my date with Pat was filling up by six-thirty. I settled down in a suitable corner to prime myself for an unpleasant interview, noting that the voices in the centre of the bar, where people drank standing, were already sufficiently loud and liberated to drown the tête-à-têtes in the plushy nooks round the walls. For the adulterous middle-class clientèle of the place, things could hardly have been ordered better.

I think Pat knew what I wanted to see her about. For the first time I could remember she was punctual for a social appointment with me, and she was dressed like a penitent in old grey slacks and a dirty white sweater. Even more telling was the ghost make-up. The effect of strain was carefully emphasized by mauve shadows.

I ordered her a double Martini. The bar specialized in large glasses, which was another reason for choosing it. *In vino veritas*. But I still hoped that Mrs Van Dopp had got the wrong end of the stick.

She tasted her drink, shivered slightly and said: 'That's the best moment, isn't it? – the way the nerves are braced by the first sip of ice-cold gin.'

I agreed. 'But I'm afraid it's the only good moment we're going to have. Do you know what I want to talk to you about?'

'Not a notion, unless it's the alibi. Don't tell me something's gone wrong with *that*?'

'You once admitted to being a congenital liar. But as far

as I know you've never lied to me about anything important. If you've lied about what happened on Friday night, we may all find ourselves in very serious trouble. . . . '

She drew on her cigarette and looked at me through the exhaled smoke. As with most instinctive women who plunge from impulse to impulse, the act of thinking was often visible on the surface, a check in the smooth endocrine flow, like a waterfall suddenly defying gravity. Then her green eyes assumed a naked woman-to-man expression, which at any other time would have given me a pang.

'David, you know me. Nobody will ever know me so well. Why should I have to start lying to you now?'

'To save yourself, or possibly Dugald. Look at me, Pat. Did you really go to Cynthia Andrei's, or did you go home to Ovington Square, thinking that you would have the house to yourselves?'

'David, I swear. Cross my heart . . . ' She stopped suddenly and gulped down half her Martini. Then she settled back against the plush settee and stared miserably out into the room.

I was determined to give her every chance to tell the truth voluntarily. I said: 'Nellie Bligh came to see me last night. She knows you sent Annie out against her will, and though she pretends to be mainly concerned with what your mother believes about Annie, I think she's sufficiently impressed with the deeper implications of this information to think in terms of mild blackmail. In other words, she wants the pension Annie would have got – either from you, as the price of not telling your mother, in which case she would probably want more: or from your mother, in which case you would have to own up.'

'She won't get a penny out of me. I'm broke. And why should I mind telling Mummy? I thought Annie needed a night out, that's all. That's *all*, I tell you. . . . '

She took a mirror out of her handbag and carefully examined her face, moving the mirror gradually closer to her right eye, then transferring it to the left as though trying another window so as to see better into herself.

Finally she dropped the mirror in her lap and put her hand on my knee. I knew then that Mrs Van Dopp was right. But that was preferable to seeing Pat strangle herself in her own lies.

'I simply had to lie, David, or you would never . . . well, I didn't dare even ask you to commit yourself to such a rotten coincidence, such a thoroughly dubious affair. You wouldn't have believed the story without checking up on it, and the whole essence of the manoeuvre was speed, don't you see?' She sighed at my wary expression. 'Now – oh I wish I had followed Dugald's advice. He kept saying that it wasn't really fair to you, that if you really . . . well, if you really were such a friend of mine, nothing would . . . '

'Pat,' I interrupted sternly, 'aren't you still being dishonest with me? Wasn't the real reason you lied that you thought I was jealous of Dugald, that I might even suspect him of being involved in the affair?' I wanted to hurt her and go on hurting her until I got the whole truth.

She looked down and said nothing for a moment; she was stroking the strap of her purse. Presently she said: 'No, you're wrong. To think that I would have to have suspected him myself, which is crazy . . . Do you think I could have another drink for the sake of my soul?'

I signalled the barman. 'Now let's have the truth, the whole truth, in as much detail as you can remember. You had planned to spend the night with Dugald, obviously?'

She nodded: 'When I start on journeys I don't bother to insure myself against loss or accident. The chances of anything going wrong were negligible.'

'You sent Annie out so that you could take Dugald home?'

'Yes.'

'And from Hans Crescent you went straight to Ovington Square?'

'Yes, but I parked the car round the corner in Knightsbridge. It did really occur to me that Desmond might have posted a private detective.'

'But you told Buxton you parked in front of the house. That's one of the relevant facts in the case.'

'So I did. Isn't that awful! But the truth would have sounded so fishy – I don't suppose it makes much difference really?'

'Okay,' I said unhappily. 'It only means that the crime could have been committed earlier or later than they think. Now let's hear the rest.'

'Of course there was no sign of Annie when we got in, and I naturally assumed she wasn't there. Even if there had been, I probably wouldn't have noticed it. I was in such a hurry to get upstairs.' A wave of the hand and a little self-deprecating gesture seemed to wish to spare me the rest. Yet she couldn't resist adding: 'I just don't know how I've managed to control myself so long with somebody I really love . . . You know what I mean? . . . Sex isn't normally such a problem between marriages. But there's something so lonely and remote about Dugald, something I felt I couldn't fathom any other way . . .'

I nodded unsympathetically and took a sip of her Martini, which was already tepid. 'And have you fathomed it now?'

'Not really. You see, it wasn't really a great success. Not to put too fine a point on it, Dugald's got a Scotch puritan streak. He didn't really want it before we were married: and I suppose that rather cramped his style. Anyway, I couldn't sleep. I was nervous and somehow depressed. I'm not good at sharing a bed at the best of times, and the ephedrine tablets made my heart beat faster, which made him restless too.

Finally, I took some sleeping tablets and he went home.'

'You sent him home, you mean?'

'He wanted me to get some sleep. "Better get it while you can," he said. "You'll have a lot of white nights in Kenya." '

'Did he suggest the sleeping tablets?'

'I can't remember: he may have done. What does it matter?'

'Just curiosity. What time was that?'

'Two o'clock. I know because I looked at my watch on the bathroom shelf.'

'Hm . . . Do you suppose there's any means of proving that – a night porter for instance, who could swear to the time he clocked in? Just in case the real story did break.'

'I imagine so. Why should the real story break?'

I didn't answer and she stared at me intensely, moving her tongue over her white teeth as though exploring for a raspberry seed. 'You didn't just *infer* that I went home, did you? . . . Christ!' Her eyes got bigger as the new situation struck her, and she bit her thumbnail till it cracked audibly. 'That VD woman – she knows something? – Paul knows something . . . '

'He knows you came home because he happened to ring you just before you got in, then again after you had disconnected your telephone: the NO ANSWER signal had changed to the ENGAGED one. I didn't mean to tell you this, but now I will, because it might be good for your soul, even better than Martinis . . . Van Dopp is a morphine addict, and now she's trying to blackmail me into supplying the stuff *ad libitum*. I've given her enough to keep her going till Wednesday, but I can't go on supplying her long without running into trouble. Addicts are tricky and, if she finds herself short, she might take it into her head to tell Buxton what she knows. . . . '

'But Paul can't do this to me! He just *can't*.'

'We're dealing with VD, not Paul. He knows absolutely nothing about it. Incidentally, he didn't breathe a word to Buxton about Friday night.'

'But he did tell that fiend ... Oh David, *darling!*' she was fairly free with her darlings, but this time I felt it was sincere. 'We'll just have to own up, that's all. I'll tell them I lied because of my divorce, then maybe they'll keep the whole thing quiet. Mummy – damn her! – probably knows the Commissioner or what-have-you. ...'

I said: 'Would you really do that, or are you just talking?'

'Of course I'll do it. I'll go and phone Scotland Yard right away.'

She got up with set, determined face, and I pulled her back into the slough of plush. I had a wild impulse to kiss her, to say that this moment was worth more than all my professional career. But instead I took her hand and raised it to my lips. It smelt of carbolic soap and nicotine.

'I just wanted to know – *for personal reasons*. Actually I think we'd be wiser to wait. If they catch the murderer soon, we may all get through safely. I can manipulate VD for a while without getting into trouble, and you've only a few days to run before your decree's made absolute.' I sighed unconvincingly. Pat looked at me searchingly. Her ghost face was worried into a special attractiveness of lines, a sketch of the soul she couldn't live up to.

'You've always had to suffer for me, haven't you? But there isn't so much I can do about it now, except to stop having you as a friend or doctor ... If only I weren't such a complete bitch!' She smiled, a small wintry contortion of the mouth, then added quickly: 'Look, why don't we get out of this dump and go and eat somewhere nice. Dugald's working on some old aunt, and Sally – poor Sally – I reckon she's used to your absences, huh?'

I said: 'Of course. She's hardened to being a doctor's wife.

I'll ring her up and tell her where we're going, in case there's a call for me. Will Mariano's be open tonight?'

In the taxi I sat firmly apart from Pat. I felt insecure, and Pat, perceiving this, couldn't forbear to make an oblique criticism of my character. As we passed the In and Out in Piccadilly, she said: 'There's a tart, a real monster, on the beat already. Did I tell you my famous escapade?'

I said: 'There are so many. Was this another of your experiments with life?'

'I just wanted to see what it was like to solicit a man. It happened just there, with the wall of the In and Out as backdrop. I had been melting into the shadows for about ten minutes, utterly disgusted by the look of all the men that passed, when one came along that looked exactly like Gary Cooper. I sidled out and trotted beside him in my highest heels, imploring him to come home with me. I believe he would have too – I looked terrific! – if a professional hadn't leapt out of the doorway, clawing at my hair and screaming at the top of her voice: "Get off my beat, you something bitch!" The next I knew was that both my rival and my pickup had completely vanished and my arm was caught in the vicelike grip of a policewoman. Imagine!...'

I shuddered audibly. 'Go on, go on. How did you escape her clutches?'

'By bursting into tears, genuine tears. I just looked up into her stern little eyes and said: "But I wasn't soliciting. I'm a respectable married woman and that man was my husband. If you take me to the station and fine me, he'll beat me again and leave me for the woman he's in love with. Oh please, please understand! I only wanted to stop him going there *tonight* – I couldn't bear it on our wedding anniversary." Would you believe it, her policewoman's heart was so touched that she let me off with a lecture about men – me!'

I was elated to be with Pat again, with a good excuse; to be so involved with her life in shaded lamplight, over a bottle of good claret and a Tournedos Sauce Béarnaise. And of course Pat took it as a personal triumph.

'David, I believe you're thinking the same as me: that if all this weren't so awful, we would be having the greatest fun in the world.'

'We're making the best of a bad job,' I said, slightly adjusting my expression. 'There's no point in being funereal, is there?'

Pat smiled secretly. 'You're always fun to be with. I've always wondered why you married Sally.'

'I married Sally because she's fun to be with too, because she's right for me, and because I love her. There! If you think anything else, it's sheer egotism on your part.'

'Egotism? The occupational disease of all attractive women. But you don't do much to cure it, do you? I don't feel your relationship with me is always as professional as it ought to be!'

'Oh, for God's sake, Pat! That's the sort of teasing you used to go in for when you were a child. I can't take it nowadays: I'm not Paul Latta.'

That went home. To my surprise she suddenly looked sad.

'Poor Paul! You may not believe it, but I'm going to miss him quite a lot. What am I going to do when I want to play?'

'Get a monkey and teach it to dance.'

'That's not funny. You think he's just a mindless puppet who can't express anything unless he's dancing? Well, that's what he is. But there's something calming about his complete lack of morals, of responsibility, of seriousness. One feels uncommitted, uninvolved in anything but the pleasure of the moment. Paul does me good.'

I said: 'I doubt if he'll do you good any more, now you've committed yourself to Dugald and his way of life. But I'm impressed by the way he's refused to do you any damage. There must be something very nice about him.'

Pat reflected a moment, then said: 'Paul would never damage me, I swear. However badly I treat him he doesn't complain, because he doesn't expect to be treated any other way. The trouble with him is that he puts up with that hag ... ' She broke off and snapped her fingers. 'I've got it! I've got it! Just let me get hold of Paul and I know how I can fix old VD. ... '

'How?'

But I had to wait three days for the answer, because at that moment the head waiter came up to me: 'Telephone for you, Dr Mortimer.'

Half an hour later I was in St John's Wood, with one of Sally's Newnham girl friends, who had been seized with a violent pain.

She was a small, bright-eyed dramatic student, who always made the mistake of thinking that because I was married to Sally I knew all about Picasso.

This time, however, she didn't waste my time. She received me with faint handshake, clasping a hot-water bottle to her abdomen. She was wearing a pitiful old nightdress and she led me in stricken silence to her bedroom.

She was remarkably coherent about her symptoms while I was taking her pulse and temperature.

'Well,' I said, 'your pulse is a bit quick, but your temperature seems normal. It can't be anything acute. Now pull up your nightdress and let's read the entrails.'

Her organs, in their thin white envelope, were eminently palpable. She lived mostly on sandwiches and black coffee, relying on her big black eyes to attract. I found no muscular rigidity.

'Does that hurt?'

'No-o.'

'That?'

'A little – well, not really.'

'That?'

'Aou, yes!' This time I had dug in ruthlessly, watching her expression carefully as I felt the junction of the caecum with the large intestine. Her eyes were cold, detached, with a hint of amusement.

'Are you sure it's just there?'

'Yes, quite positive.'

'But when I did that before, you said it didn't hurt. Just lie and rest for a minute, then I'll get *you* to tell *me* where you feel the pain.'

I handed her a cigarette and lit it for her. I waited a minute by my watch before I spoke. 'Now tell me.'

She poked herself doubtfully. 'Well, I'm not sure now. I suppose it could have been just colic.'

I said: 'I'll tell you what we'll do. Your appendix may be lying in a little pouch, impossible to examine except rectally. Come tomorrow and I'll do it. It's a bit unpleasant, but not really painful. If that proves negative, I'll send you to Galbraith. You've probably got a grumbling appendix and he'll probably want to yank it out, but there's no better surgeon in the country.'

That worked like a charm. 'No,' she said, 'I'd rather leave it till after Christmas. The truth is I began to feel better very soon after I telephoned your house, but too late to stop you coming. I'm afraid you think me rather a fraud, dragging you from a dinner date for nothing.'

'Not a bit,' I said, adding maliciously: 'It must have been Sally who told you to call me, and she's very learned about symptoms.'

It was midnight by the time I got home. Sally, who had been drinking by herself, made no attempt to deny the trick she had played on me. Nor had she any doubts about the ethics of it. 'I'm not like you,' she said calmly, 'I've a single set of ethics in my life, not one for medicine and one for marriage. If I interrupted your conversation at a vital point, I'm sorry. But by that time you had had five hours alone with Pat. I should have thought two would have been enough, if all you wanted from her was the truth.'

I poured myself a stiff drink. Our rare quarrels were always pepped up by drink: we agreed it was easier to do it properly. Hard, necessary things were said. But afterwards, when relations improved, we could always blame the alcohol.

'All right,' I said. 'We'll skip the ethics of sending doctors on wild-goose chases on Sunday night. But I can't for the life of me understand why you chose that moment to be jealous. You and I and Pat and Dugald are all in grave danger of public scandal, if not of prosecution. And you know quite well that everything depends on our keeping in close touch with one another . . . well, don't you?'

Sally's smile was surprisingly bitter. I had never seen her look quite like that before. She said: 'I know it's all a wonderful excuse for keeping "in close touch" with Pat. Don't deceive yourself, David, and you won't deceive me. From my point of view there are *two* grave dangers, and I'm not sure I don't prefer scandal and ruin.'

'But it's natural for Pat and me to talk things over. We understand each other: you and Dugald don't. And where's the danger anyway? You said yourself that Dugald and Pat seemed to be very much in love.'

'Being in love with Dugald, if she really is, wouldn't prevent Pat from enjoying your being in love with her. Did you really think it fair to me, knowing I know you're in love with Pat, to insist on taking her to a restaurant after I had besought you to bring her to dinner here?'

'But I told you why. In front of you she would never have

told the truth about what happened the night of Annie's murder. Pat doesn't talk to other women. . . . ' I sat down beside her and put my arm round her shoulders. I am amazed, looking back on this scene, how injured I felt, how little I understood Sally's feeling of insecurity.

I said: 'I'm sorry, darling, but it never occurred to me this would hurt you. Pat and I have always been close friends – you know that. But it's a brother-and-sister relationship. What on earth makes you think I'm *in love* with her?'

She drew away from me suddenly, pushing with her legs till her back came up rigid against the arm of the sofa. She sat there for a moment, bolt upright, staring at me with an odd expression, as though I had receded suddenly into a new perspective.

'The first time you told me you were in love with Pat was the night of our wedding anniversary . . . you don't remember? No, of course you don't. You said it in your sleep after we had made love!'

For a moment I sat shattered and silent. Was I really in love with Pat? Was all this talk of brother-and-sister relationship a monstrous piece of self-deception? I am ashamed to record that, even as I was eating this humble pie, the thought of Pat and the policewoman flitted like a bat through my attic storey, making nonsense of wedding anniversaries.

Sally, seeing my deeper reaction, pursued relentlessly: 'The second time was the night after the murder, after I had come in and found you and Pat on the sofa. You spoke to me. You said wonderful things. And it was only when you had called me Pat that I realized you were again talking in your sleep. . . . '

'Jesus!' I said. Then, rallying on a wave of angry self-justification: 'It's just like you to seize on Freudian slips and try to twist them into real infidelities. Love, as I've always understood it, involves the whole being. It doesn't just creep out at night, when the Censor's tired out. Or does it?'

'I don't know, David. I just don't know. All I'm certain of at this moment is that Pat's trying to alienate your affections – for what purpose, except sheer devilry, I simply can't imagine. Maybe she doesn't know what she's doing. But I have to act as though she does. I beg of you to examine yourself as you examine other people. . . . Now please give me another drink and tell me what she told you about last Friday. . . . '

Sally listened impassively. But the final note, the bass tuba let loose by an irresponsible organist, shook her consciousness to the foundations.

'Good Heavens,' she exclaimed, 'have you thought what Pat may mean by "fixing" Van Dopp? How can you "fix" a blackmailer except by counter-blackmail *or worse*? What you still don't realize, darling, is that your childhood playmate lives in a semi-criminal world: her ways are crooked, and so are her emotions.'

She was still embroidering this theme when the telephone shrilled.

'You take it,' I said. 'I'm feeling too drunk.'

Sally said: 'Hullo-o?' Then: 'Oho,' and turned to me, putting her hand over the receiver: 'SHE wants to talk to you.'

Pat said: 'David, what on earth's up with Sally? . . . No, of course he can't answer, you fool! (Sorry, I was only talking to myself). Look now, David, this is urgent. You said you were seeing VD on Wednesday – right? . . . Well, don't keep the appointment. Ring her up and say you've considered her case carefully and have decided you can only treat her if she really wants to be disintoxicated. . . . What? . . . No, there's no danger. You've just got to trust me, that's all. Good night.'

Chapter 8

The Arms of Morpheus

ON Wednesday morning I tried to telephone Mrs Van Dopp. There was no reply, so I rang the hall porter at Cathedral Mansions and asked if she had gone away. 'Not to my knowledge, sir,' he said darkly. 'It could be she's not answering today, but that's just a guess.'

Clearly he knew too much to commit himself to strangers on the telephone. He probably thought I was a dope-pedlar. At any rate his information was sufficient to bring me round straight away.

He was sitting in the lift, a beery-looking old-soldier type, half-heartedly polishing brass, with one eye on the sporting page of the *Daily Mirror*, which was spread out beside him on the seat. 'Third floor,' he said, when I told him who I wanted. 'Would it be you that telephoned by any chance . . . sir?' The 'sir' came after a second's scrutiny. He had probably decided against my being a dope-pedlar. I was more like an officer from the Narcotics Squad. 'Okay, sir, I'll run you up.'

'She's in, all right,' he confided, as the lift came to a stand-still. 'Do you happen to know the lady well?'

'Not well. I'm a doctor. She asked me to call.'

'Ah –' his eye rested dubiously on my bag – 'I'll wait here for you in case she don't answer.'

The bell probed through the flat. I tried again and again, without result. He stepped out of the lift and joined me on the landing. 'If you ask me, sir,' he said conspiratorially, 'she's

75

in no condition to answer your ring. It isn't the first time I've seen gentlemen ring and go away.'

'But her son? She has a son, hasn't she? I understand he looked after her.'

'Mr Latta, eh?' He winked knowingly. 'Ah, there's a fine night-bird for you! He 'opped it yesterday supper-time. Can't say I blame 'im neither: I never met a more quarrelsome lady.'

'Do you mean to say he's left her for good?' I asked, keeping my finger pressed on the bell.

'Well, he left with two suitcases. Told me he'd taken a job down in Maidenhead and didn't know when he'd be back. Gentlemen like Mr Latta don't leave the nest unless it's fouled up good and proper.'

I took my finger off the bell and said quickly: 'I've got to get into this flat somehow. Have you got a master key?'

He produced a key-ring from his waistcoat pocket and stood there looking hesitant.

'Don't worry,' I said, 'I'll take full responsibility.'

A light was burning in the curtained hall and there was a coppery glow from the passage leading to the living-room. 'Mrs Van Dopp,' the porter called. Then, more loudly: 'Mrs Van Dopp, here's the doctor come to see you.'

There was no answer and I hurried down the passage with the porter just behind me. The living-room door was wide open, and I was half-way there when I caught sight of her. She was sitting back in her armchair, facing me, and as I moved forward the light of the reading lamp on the table beside her was suddenly reflected up from the glass top, so that I had the vivid illusion of having startled her from a deep narcotic drowse amid pale arabesques of wrought iron and dim echoes of mirrored light . . .

'Mrs Van Dopp . . . ' I began, then stopped and stared,

meeting the hypnotic stare of enormous black pupils, fixed apparently in an anguish of terror. The half-open mouth was a black rictus underlining the expression of living horror. But the ghastly hue of the cyanosed lips made it all too plain that Death was only imitating Life. From the grey roots of Mrs Van Dopp's straggling hair, the blue colour spread downwards, broken by the sheen of grey silk pyjamas, to emerge more vividly on the bare, emaciated forearm that lay across the arm of her chair: the hand, palm uppermost, was directly under the lampshade, and it looked as though it had been dipped in blue ink . . .

'Get the police at once. Ask for Chief Inspector Buxton, C.I.D. And tell him I'm here – Doctor Mortimer . . . Go on, man, don't stand there goggling. You'd better use the telephone in the hall.'

The only reason for this last injunction was that I wanted to be alone with my blackmailer, who was now, for a moment at least, my patient. Not that I had any need to determine the cause of death. She had been dead many hours. Stale scent, which suggested to me the fetidness of opium, still hung about her like a living exhalation. I had to find out, and quickly, how the dose had been administered.

Three things held my attention, knowing something about her case history. The first was the emptiness of the little bottle of morphine I had given her, for safety's sake, from the reserve I had brought back from Normandy in the war. The second was the barely perceptible mark on the barrel of the hypodermic lying beside the bottle . . . That suggested that she hadn't injected more than the equivalent of two and a half grains of morphia; not enough to kill off an addict accustomed to two grains a day.

The third thing that interested me – and this was even more puzzling – was the site she had chosen for the injection. I didn't tumble to this at first. I wasted a whole minute examining her shrunken thighs, trying to find traces of a fresh prick. This was where she habitually pricked herself, often carelessly and in a desperate hurry, through her clothes. The flesh was covered with little ulcer scars due to lack of asepsis. It didn't occur to me to look at her arm, till the porter, back from ringing Scotland Yard, suddenly stood over me and exclaimed: 'Blimey!' I turned to see what was the matter and found him staring at the corpse, fascinated. 'I've 'eard of a blue baby,' he announced in a hoarse whisper, 'but never 'eard of a *blue lady*. She's all blue like the veins had burst.'

That gave me the idea of examining the bend of her elbow. And there, sure enough, was a purplish clot of blood. I was about to pull up her sleeve again when I noticed something strange. Could it be a highlight round the sore place on the vein? No, surely not there, in the concavity of the elbow. I couldn't flex the arm because of *rigor mortis*. So I focused the reading-lamp on the place till I was satisfied I hadn't made a mistake. In life she had been personally dirty and I had remarked on it three days ago, advising her to swab her skin with alcohol before using the needle.

Would she have followed my advice if she had intended to kill herself?

'So she did herself in?' – The porter's voice at my elbow was husky. He couldn't stop staring at her. 'She must have done it on account of him leaving her.'

I said: 'That's for the police to decide. But it looks like it.'

'Do you see the look in her eyes! Blimey! I saw some 'orrible sights when Jerry first used gas on us – but this!' He shuddered and looked away. . . . 'Well, if you won't be needing me any more . . . '

I said: 'I'd rather you waited till the police arrive. We can go into the hall and have a smoke.'

As we left the room my eye caught the amber gleam of a half-empty glass standing on the bar. But at the moment all I thought was: 'If it weren't for the porter, I'd go and get myself a stiff one.'

The Home Office man was the first to arrive, a distinguished chap wearing a pearl tiepin and spats. In my practice patients invariably died in their beds, so I wasn't used to pathologists. I had always thought of them as the kites of my profession, hovering in the hope of a corpse, then rushing in to flay the flesh and pickle the poisoned bits in jars. I detected the faint odour of formalin vying with the brilliantine on his hair, and it struck me that his rather brittle colleague-to-colleague manner could have been due to a need to compensate for his unsavoury profession. I was wrong.

'Yes,' he said, 'the pupils do sometimes relax *post mortem*.' He straightened up from the body to examine the little rubber-capped bottle. 'Strong stuff, eh? It's amazing that six years after the war there's still so much of it floating around. Some of those R.A.M.C. orderlies must have made a fortune peddling.'

I noted the innuendo. I was to feel I was a doctor, above suspicion of providing the poison. This honour among doctors was a pleasant part of my profession, but I had never appreciated it so much as now. I couldn't believe he hadn't noticed the same thing as I had yet. His examination had seemed extraordinarily casual, as if to say: 'I'll take it from you all's above board.'

A heavy tread sounded in the passage, Buxton arriving on the scene of the crime. 'Well, well, Mortimer,' – he seemed delighted to see me, despite the inauspicious occasion – 'Our lives are converging with a vengeance.'

He stood gazing at the unpleasant spectacle in the lamplight.

'So this is, or rather was, the lady who lived with Mr Latta. I didn't have the pleasure of meeting her the other day.'

I said: 'I would put it that he lived with her. I gather from our friend here that Mr Latta has just left her to take a job in Maidenhead. That may have some bearing on her suicide.'

He questioned the hall porter for a minute, then turned to me again. 'So she was a patient of yours? . . . I say, can't we have some light on all this? *You* – draw the curtains, will you.'

The porter drew the curtains, and Mrs Van Dopp appeared even deader in the grey morning light. Paul's picture looked on without emotion.

'She called me in a few days ago,' I was saying. 'She told me she was suffering agony from an old gall-bladder operation. But she was obviously suffering from withdrawal symptoms. I gave her a shot and warned her she couldn't go on being my patient unless she promised to try and undertake a cure. She agreed to – as soon as her family troubles were settled.'

'So you think there's no doubt it was suicide?'

'None at all,' I lied; and the pathologist, prowling, suddenly turned and asked me: 'By the way, how much of the stuff was she taking? You ought to know her tolerance level.'

'Two to two and a half grains – she hadn't been on it very long and I believe she could have been cured. I gave her slightly less on Sunday night. I thought I could keep her going on stabilising doses, but she may have felt worse than I knew, in view of her family worries.'

'Okay.' The pathologist scribbled in his notebook. 'Well, the autopsy will show what she's got in her stomach. But, judging from what you say, I would expect to find about ten grains in her. Suicide, no doubt about it. She just squirted the whole bottle into the main line and sank blissfully into the arms of Morpheus.'

Buxton asked: 'Did she tell you exactly what her worries

were? I mean, you automatically ask that sort of thing, don't you?'

'I asked her, but I didn't get any clear answer. I didn't want to get too tough with her the first time, particularly as she had promised to reform. But my guess is that her son had threatened to leave her unless she took a cure, and that that merely made her want more dope – a vicious circle.'

Buxton nodded understandingly. He felt for his pipe, thought better of it, and accepted a cigarette from the pathologist's silver case. I had the impression that both of them were thoroughly relaxed. The suicides of dope-addicts were no doubt relatively uninteresting – to be written off without much investigation.

'All right,' Buxton told the porter, 'get those removal boys up from the hall. I'll just take a look round the flat and make sure there's no letter. By the way, Mortimer, aren't I lunching with you at the Wildman today? . . . Good, then I don't suppose you'll want to hang around here any longer. I may have some interesting things to tell you by then.'

The pathologist looked rather impressed. As I left he was putting the syringe and morphine bottle into envelopes. . . .

When I got out into the fresh air, I filled my lungs and started thinking dark thoughts. I stopped at Victoria and hurried into a telephone booth.

I got Mrs Tatham, who told me that Pat was still in the bath, reading probably, and running the water. She hadn't been able to get a bath herself, and it would be a pleasure to switch the call through. 'Keep ringing,' she said, 'until she answers.'

Finally I got Pat: 'Listen to my teeth chattering. My mother took all the hot water. Just a second till I shake the icicles off.'

'Pat,' I said, 'what did you mean about "fixing" Mrs Van Dopp?'

'Why, what's happened?... My God! She hasn't gone to the police, has she? Paul said that was just talk...'

'Will you please answer my question first.'

'Well, you know – or perhaps you don't – that Mrs Van Dopp absolutely depends on Paul. My plan was to get him to scare the old creature out of this blackmailing racket by threatening to walk out on her. Actually he's often threatened to do this, if she wouldn't give up dope. But when it came to it, he never had the guts to act, because that would have meant his giving up his allowance and plunging into the struggle for existence. And of course VD knew it. So this time I thought I'd strengthen his hand by getting Dickie Syme to offer him a temporary job as a gigolo in the River Club at Maidenhead. Dickie agreed, provided I paid the wages on the sly and that he had no obligation to keep Paul on a day longer than he pulled his weight on the dance-floor. Of course Paul was tickled to death by the proposal. He was furious with her anyway for trying to do this thing to me.'

'To *me*,' I corrected. 'Well, you've certainly succeeded in shutting her up. She's dead.'

Pat whistled down the telephone. 'Do you mean she's killed herself?'

'That's what the police think. Do you know if she ever threatened to commit suicide?'

'No... Actually I believe she did once. But Paul thought it was all bluff – just a means of enslaving him for ever. He'll never forgive himself for this.'

That was one weight off my mind. But there remained another, equally heavy. As I went round visiting my patients that morning, I kept seeing Mrs Van Dopp's corpse and the clean patch on her inner elbow. Its implications were so frightening that I had to keep reminding myself of the police surgeon's words – 'suicide, no doubt about it'. I had to keep telling myself that she had died easily, though death had made such a horrible waxwork of her; and that the world was better off without her – not to mention Paul, Sally and me, Pat and Dugald.

The final irony of the 'fixing' of Mrs van Dopp was revealed to me by Buxton at the Wildman Club.

By the time I got there, ten minutes late, he was already behaving like one of the elect. He had found himself another Carthusian in the smoking-room and had accepted a gin and Italian. 'Here's my host,' he told his schoolmate, 'I expect you two know each other . . . You don't? Well, I'll be jiggered . . . . This is Mortimer of Pageites – Wreford of Weekites.'

He radiated self-satisfaction. Even when I managed to tear him away from Wreford, a stockbroker I had been avoiding for years, I couldn't get him off the subject of Charterhouse. He made no reference whatever to our meeting that morning. Nor did he mention the Ovington Square murder. Once, when his flow of schoolday reminiscence was interrupted, I tried putting out a shy feeler: 'Well, how's crime?' The answer was: 'On the increase, worse luck. I can't tell you what a pleasure it is to get away from it and talk about other things.' His real pleasure, I suspected, was keeping me in suspense.

After lunch I asked him if he had time for coffee and brandy.

'Why, yes – if there's some quiet place where we can have a chin-wag.'

As we crossed the hall a page came up to me: 'Chief-Inspector Buxton wanted on the phone, sir.' The boy's face was radiant. But Hardwicke, the neurologist, who was on his way out, turned and touched me on the arm. 'Collaborator!' he hissed. '*Mortimer au poteau!*'

When my guest had finished telephoning, I took him up to the library, explaining that the place was completely disused, except by misogynists on Bank Holidays. It was dim up there and there was no fire. But we had had plenty to drink and the room was charming – the last in the Wildman to resist all modernization. Sir Humphry Davy had warmed his bottom in front of the Adam mantelpiece while he brooded about potassium. Smollett had sat at the big writing-desk, dashing off a petulant letter to a Sea Lord about sanitation in Ships of the Line.

Amid all this history, surrounded by Chippendale book-cases inviolate for years, Chief-Inspector Buxton pricked his cigar with a two-inch nail that had been used – he told me proudly – in a recent teenage gang-murder. Then he said:

'I can tell you now, *in the strictest confidence*, that the Ovington Square business is in the bag. Yes, sir, in the bag. I'm afraid the arrest will be a blow to our mutual friend, Lady Killaloe.'

He stuck his cigar in his mouth and lit it. In the flare of the match his dull, grey eyes seemed to bulge from their sockets: they were like binoculars fixed on my face . . .

I wasn't sure what reaction he hoped to produce. But his ponderous approach warned me to keep my hand well up. It went up, I now realize, a second too late.

'Well, blow me down!' I chose a phrase that seemed suitably Old Boy. 'I congratulate you on a splendid piece of work.' I hesitated before asking: 'I'm sure Lady Killaloe will feel the same as I do, even if this means that you've arrested her protégée.'

If he was disappointed he didn't show it. 'Well, Mollie Rideout was suspect from the beginning, because of the de Hartung job in Mount Street. And as you may or may not know she visited Lady Killaloe on the afternoon of the murder.'

'You're surely not suggesting that she did it?'

'Of course not. But she could have been the brains (if there were any) behind the robbery. The executive was her kid bro, who's been trailing around for at least a year with a band of juvenile mobsters. He made the mistake of boasting to one of his mates in Pimlico, and though these young thugs play the game strictly according to the rules of the Underworld, we've got police Scouts mixing with them, and we soon got wind of it. By that time Syd had skipped, got a job as a bellhop in a Southend hotel, and it took us twenty-four hours to trace him. At this stage we were only "anxious to interview him", as the phrase goes. All we'd found in the Rideout flat was a mask and a pair of gloves, which are standard playtime equipment for these high-minded teenagers. All we had against him was that he was Mollie's brother and that his behaviour had been incriminating. He was scared stiff when he found himself in my office. He denied any knowledge of the Ovington Square job. He even denied boasting to a friend that he'd done it. He said the friend had quarrelled with him over a girl and must have made up the story to get him into trouble. Well, I couldn't prove that he was lying, but I was very struck by the story he was alleged to have confided to his friend; it was remarkably detailed as regards the killing of the old nurse and it confirmed my original theory that the murderer had gone on hitting her because he knew she had recognized him. He had even described the look in Annie's eyes when he put his hand over her mouth – "They screamed for mercy". That made a great impression on the other boy. . . . Anyway, to cut a long story short, I let Syd go. I might even have dropped him as a suspect if I hadn't caught one of my colleagues laughing quietly up his sleeve. I don't like being laughed at. Last night, just to make sure, I took a couple of men to Mollie's flat and searched the place methodically. I found what I was looking for in the girl's bedroom – eighteen inches of lead piping, inserted into a hollow brass rod in the hanging-cupboard. It had been carefully wiped: no blood, no hairs, no fingerprints. But the plumber who was working at Ovington Square has positively identified it as the missing length. . . . '

I took advantage of the pause to ask: 'But the jewellery? If you can't find any of that, I should have thought your case against either of the Rideouts was thin?'

'Oh, I forgot to say about the telephone call that just came through. A bracelet of Mrs Tatham's was found this morning in a laurel bush in Chelsea Gardens: it was close to the railings, within a stone's throw of the Pimlico Road, where the Rideouts hang out. It could have been flung there from a window of a taxi or bus.'

I said: 'Then you think you've got enough to arrest them?'

'The boy, yes. But conspiracy's harder to prove and I like to get my cases neatly tied up. You'd be surprised how often good police work gets sabotaged by a clever defence and twelve honest dunderheads.'

I said: 'If I were defending in this case, I would begin by asking myself how Mollie Rideout, knowing she was bound to be suspected, could have imagined she could get away with it?'

Buxton chuckled, a deep viscerotonic chuckle. 'I'm afraid you credit the criminal classes with more general intelligence than they really have: they're specialists, you see. However, these birds haven't been charged yet, and if you feel like it why don't you try doing a bit of preliminary work for the Defence? That boy's going to need a great deal of defending. . . . '

I looked at him in amazement. 'What is this? A detective, about to make an arrest in an important murder case, whose career partly depends on a conviction, opens the field to a mere member of the public? Am I drunk, or are you?'

Again the chuckle. 'Well, we've certainly had a good lunch, one of the pleasantest I've ever had. But you've got me wrong, Mortimer – I suspect you always have since the day when I got you beaten for talking in prep. I've a good memory, you know, and I remember how you looked at me when you were bending over the chair at the end of the room, after the head monitor had given you the first whack. You thought me a sadist, didn't you? You think I'm a sadist still: that I only care about convictions and promotion. Well, I'll tell you something I wouldn't have told you if you hadn't treated me so decently. I didn't like seeing you beaten: I don't like what's coming to these wretched Rideouts. But justice is justice, and I want you to see that's what I care about. Go and see these people, have a talk with them. Then come back and tell me if I'm wrong!'

A sentimental man? A tormented man? Or a remarkably intuitive policeman? I never expected to get a categorical answer.

Chapter 9

A Gentleman from the *Scots Pictorial*

'So that's that!' Sally said. 'Van Dopp's in the morgue, Syd's in his cell, God's in his heaven and . . , Ah, here it is in black and white – "Youth Questioned in connection with Knightsbridge Murder". The Stop Press says he's been *detained.*'

While I was reading, she sat on the floor beside me. 'Dinner's ready when we are. Let's get mulled and talk. Oh, David. I'm so happy it's all over?'

I didn't miss the faint question-mark, the need for re-assurance. She wanted to hear: 'Now Pat can get on with her marriage and disappear out of our lives. Soon she'll be five thousand miles away, and meanwhile I've no desire to go on seeing her.' What she got was: 'I'm afraid it's very far from over. I'm certain Buxton's on the wrong track.'

'But the evidence sounds overwhelming.'

'Too overwhelming. Take one point among many. Why should Syd hide the weapon in the flat? Considering where he lives the obvious place for disposing of it was the river.'

'Perhaps he wanted to keep it as a souvenir. Surely the police know more than you do about abnormal criminal psychology?'

'They know so much about it that they can't see the bonnet for the bees. . . . But I haven't told you the strangest part of my talk with Buxton. *He actually suggested my going to see Mollie!* The reason he gave was that he wants me to convince myself he isn't just out to get a conviction: he wants to be thought high-minded, public school!'

88

'Sounds to me like a phoney reason.'

'To me too . . . But I'm not sure. He's a queer chap.'

Sally frowned at her thoughts. 'Please, darling, *please* leave it alone. If anybody can do anything for the Rideouts, it's Pat. If she really cares about them, she can employ a private detective. You've got your practice to look after.'

'I'm afraid it's too late to cry off now. I rang Mollie at her dress-shop this afternoon, and she'll be waiting for me at her flat after dinner.'

Sally made one last appeal: '*Must* you stir all this up again just when it seemed to be settling down? Don't you ever think of me?'

I thought that bordered on cynicism.

Mollie lived on the Eleven bus-route where it turns left out of Lower Sloane Street and heads for Victoria. Her flat, over a bicycle shop in the main road, was accessible by a side-door in a dirty little cul-de-sac. Almost opposite the door was the entrance to the saloon bar of the Coldstream, a faded monument to the craze for ornate tile-mosiacs touched off by Ruskin's *Stones of Venice*. As I pushed open Mollie's door, I looked across the alley and saw the crouching silhouettes of drinkers gathered round pin-tables near the bar window. Written across them in translucence was BURTONS. The rest of the window was opaque.

I began to appreciate what Pat saw in Mollie as soon as the light went on at the head of the stairs and she stood there softly welcoming me. 'Is it you, Doctor Mortimer? I'm so glad. Now mind the steps, the lino's slippery.' It was the whisper of one trained in the subterfuges of Pat's secret life in the suspicious atmosphere of Mrs Tatham's mansion. I had come to help her: she made me feel like a conspirator.

I followed her into the little sitting-room. She turned and saw the surprise on my face. 'It's ever so simple, really. But

Lady Killaloe used to come here often. She helped me with the furnishing.'

'It's gay and comfortable. I can imagine she liked coming here.' I was thinking how Mollie's remark reflected one of Pat's most endearing qualities. I could imagine her dropping in to see Mollie without a trace of constraint or condescension, just being one young woman with another. Her feeling that employees were at least as good as her had been at the root of the trouble about the jade earrings. 'And who does Mollie Rideout think she is?' Mrs Tatham had asked. To which Pat retorted: 'She's in a better position to know than *I* am!'

'But she hasn't been up to see me since . . . ' Mollie was saying. She broke off to take the cigarette I was offering her. 'Thanks, I will. They seem to settle you when the nerves are on edge.'

'Since the police started visiting you, you mean?'

She nodded and took a quick automatic look to see what brand of cigarettes they were.

'That's why I was surprised when you rang me, knowing you and she were such friends, as it were.'

'Oh-o?' I couldn't help smiling at the 'as it were'. 'How did you know we were such friends? I'm the family doctor, so I know all of them quite well.'

'Lady Killaloe told me a lot of things. She trusted me, because I never let her down, you see. And she never let me down either. She's been lovely to me – up till now she has . . . '

'What's happened now?'

'Well, after the police came asking questions about Syd, I tried phoning her several times. But they always said she wasn't at home. Yesterday, when they found the lead piping, I thought "blow the expense", and took a taxi round to Ovington Square. Very sorry, they said, her Ladyship's not at home; though her car was standing in front of the house!'

'Who were "they"?'

'Cumberledge, the mouldy old stuffed shirt. He never did like me: thought I was too familiar with her Ladyship. They were all the same except Annie – poor love.'

She sat forward, staring into the gas fire, her neatly tousled head cradled in well-kept, capable hands, whose fingers drummed on her temples. She was wearing a low-cut black *lamé* frock that had had its première, I surmised, on Pat. She looked undersized in it, but overdressed.

'Then it's "they," I'm sure, who are preventing you from seeing Lady Killaloe. She's very fond of you and I'm sure she'll do everything she can to help you.'

'I don't know,' she said miserably, 'I just don't believe in anybody any more. . . . Of course it was Mrs Tatham who put the police on us. She knew all about Syd going round there and creating, the day after I got the sack.'

'Ah! What sort of a scene did he make?'

'He told Mrs Cumberledge – she's the cook, you know – that one day he'd get his revenge on the mistress.'

'Then it isn't surprising they suspected him, is it? But whatever they say about the boy, he seems to have some decent instincts.'

'That's right, he has. He's got a good heart, really. But he never had a chance, you see – what with no father, Mum being an alcoholic, and being evacuated during the war. When Mum died and he went to live with his auntie in Stepney, he ran wild with the other boys on the street.'

'I thought he lived with you?'

'Only since I left the job at Ovington Square. Auntie wouldn't keep him any longer, you see, not even with me contributing. She thought him as bad as he made himself out, romancing about girls and razor fights and about the police being after him. He's seen too many crime movies, and he makes up for being weedy and backward at school by pretending to be a big shot, a leader. I thought he'd be better off living with me. But he soon got in with a gang of Teddy boys round Victoria, and they played him up, started calling him Syd the slasher, just to take the mike out of him. That made him desperate. . . .'

'Then what makes you so sure he had nothing to do with the business at Ovington Square?'

'He told me he didn't. Besides, if he'd really done it, he wouldn't have skipped down to Southend like he did. He just wanted his gang to think the police were after him; thought he might get something in the papers.'

'Then what about the lead pipe and the bracelet? How did they get where they did?'

'Ask the police . . . ' She stopped and stared with big suspicious eyes: the greasy make-up on her eyelids made her face look at once dewy and old. . . . 'Hey! There was nothing in the papers about that. Who told *you*, I'd like to know?'

'I was told in confidence by a detective I happen to know. That's why I've come, to help you find out how and when you were framed.'

'If you ask me, the police did the framing. That was the only way they could get a case against Syd.'

I said: 'If you know what's good for you, don't start accusing the police. Now think hard: could anybody have got into this flat while you were away at your job?' I got up and walked over to the window. The lights of the Coldstream lit the little alley.

'Nobody could have broken in,' she was saying. 'With the pub right opposite, they wouldn't dare.'

'Have you had any visitors, apart from the police?'

'Nobody except the reporter from the *Scots Pictorial* and he was ever such a nice gentleman; rang up the shop first and asked if I'd mind him calling on me. All he wanted was a few details about Lady Killaloe's life – you know, how she

dresses, what she has for breakfast, where she buys her
lingerie. . . . '

'And did you give him what he asked for?'

'Well, there wasn't any harm, was there? – especially since
it was Lady Killaloe herself who told him to come to me.'

I controlled my surprise. 'What did he look like?'

'Like an intellectual, I should say. He had a moustache
and a little beard and he wore glasses. He was very kind and
considerate. He went over to the pub and bought some beer,
and afterwards he offered to pay me for the interview, but of
course I wouldn't take money for that!'

'Did you leave him alone in the room at all?'

'No-o.'

'He didn't ask you for anything? – an aspirin, for instance,
or a glass of water? . . . No? . . . And you didn't have to go and
powder your nose?'

'Of course not, Doctor Mortimer!'

'Why "of course not"? I'm a doctor, Mollie, and you don't
have to be coy with me. Are you quite sure you didn't have to
powder your nose?'

I could see she was profoundly shaken.

'To tell the truth, I don't know what was wrong with me
that night: I could hardly sit still.'

'Did you drink much beer?'

'Only one glass, just to keep him company.'

'Ah' – I was thinking of a trick the students used to play at
mixed parties. It had been the cause of one of my worst
quarrels with Pat, and for months after the fatal party she
had refused to believe I was entirely innocent. But time had
mellowed the memory into one of her funniest doubtful
stories, and there were few among her friends nowadays who
hadn't heard and repeated it among their friends. . . .

'Where's your lavatory?' I abruptly asked Mollie.

She looked embarrassed again. 'We got the place so inexpensively, you see. It's central, and in some ways ever so convenient. . . . '

'Where's your lavatory?' I repeated, so sternly that she answered straight as to the manner born: 'Ground floor, behind the stairs, where we keep the coal.'

'Could this man have known the geography of the house?'

She was with me at last, puzzled but eager. 'Not before, he couldn't. But he asked where he could wash his hands when he was on his way down to fetch the beer.'

I had only two more questions to ask her. I was convinced that only a woman – and an innocent one – would have been panicked into throwing a valuable bracelet into the unlikely place where it had been found. But I decided to leave that question for the more important one: 'Did you tell the police about this journalist?'

'Of course I did. But after the way they treated me, like a criminal, I wasn't going to give myself away to them, not likely!' Her mouth narrowed and pursed at the recollection. 'After all, I have my pride.'

I came out of Mollie's whistling to myself. I opened the door and looked across the alley. The silhouettes were still there behind the window, and I hurried across, pushing the door open quickly. Two soldiers were rattling and banging at the pin-table in the window embrasure and, behind them, in the window seat, was a civilian nursing a tankard of beer. As I ordered my beer, from a fat, female publican with a shawl, I caught his eye in the mirror behind the bar. It wasn't the sort of eye one could catch except by accident. I had only a second to note the long canine face before it burrowed back into a newspaper. But that glimpse was enough to warn me not to gossip with the publican.

I drank my beer quickly and went out. There was a cold wind blowing down the alley and a cigarette packet rustled along the concrete, fetching up against Mollie's garbage can. No doubt the police had poked their noses into that.

I turned right into the street and sauntered along to the bus-stop, then stood back into the doorway of a fruiterer's. It was quiet for the moment, and the diffused rumble of traffic from busier districts seemed to particularize the quick beat of footsteps. He stood at the corner, and after glancing up and down the street, decided that I must be at the bus-stop. He was so sure of it that he didn't bother to glance into the recess where I stood: he merely leant against the lamp-post with his back to me and went on reading his paper. But when Number Eleven came along, he waited for me to climb aboard before swinging himself on to the platform. I jumped off when the bus was doing about twenty and fell heavily into the gutter. Then I walked back to the pub.

'What, back again already?' The woman drew her shawl over her shoulders and looked at me with genial interest. 'A pint of bitter? All right, dear.'

I took a long swig. 'I suppose the people here are mostly from the barracks?'

'Oh yes, it's convenient for the boys. But we've been getting some queer customers lately!'

I smiled understandingly: 'Well, I'm not one of them. That's to say I'm a newshawk. I'm interested in the girl opposite.'

'She's a nice little thing. Quite particular too – you don't see her taking in men at night. But that kid brother of hers –' she sniffed significantly – 'well, I suppose we're all handi-capped one way or another.'

She leant her bosom on the bar and I saw her handicap. He was bleary, unshaven, moving a crate of beer behind the bar.

She said: 'My husband says I didn't ought to talk to strangers. You never know who they are. Are you from the *Mirror* or the *Express*?'

'From the *Express* – we're so quick off the mark that we get there before the crime's been committed!'

She smiled and waved a fat finger at me. 'You're not first this time. She had a gentleman in two nights ago and he wasn't from the Yard, I can tell you: a copper wouldn't have come over for bottled beer. He looked like a journalist: bit rough, you know.'

'What kind of beer did he order?'

'Stingoes – he said he liked them short and strong.'

'Then it must have been old Callahan from the *News of the World*. Trust him to get in on the ground floor. Was he clean-shaven, with a little toothbrush moustache?'

'No, bearded, with glasses. From Scotland, seemingly.'

'Hm . . . I wonder who he could have been. I know one or two in Fleet Street who might fit that description. Anything else you remember about him? Any mannerisms?'

She thought for a moment. 'Well, not really . . . wait a minute though, he did seem a bit impatient and nervous while my husband was getting up a new crate of Stingoes. He kept doing like this' – she pulled awkwardly at a pendulous earlobe and a heavy glass peardrop fell on to the bar between us. . . .

There was a long silence broken by a click. Then the quavering agitated voice of Elvis Presley broke into the rhythm of a rock and roll. A young soldier stood in front of the jukebox, tapping with his feet and swaying his hips.

'Well, thanks, I must be going. Keep the change.' I left her staring at the ten-bob note, bewildered by the sudden ways of journalists.

I took a bus to Sloane Square. The man in front of me was reading *The Economist* and his face was just visible over it, mirrored in the driver's back. But I didn't become interested in his face until he let the paper drop with a sigh and started pulling reflectively at his right ear. What then struck me was the ordinariness of that business face, and the probability that at least fifty per cent of all Englishmen did something similar in moments of anxiety or mental abstraction. Though the percentage of ear-pullers was probably small compared with that of the nail-biters, chin-strokers and hair-twisters, I had been warned about jumping to conclusions.

But was I jumping to conclusions? The man had spoken with a Scots accent; he was one of Pat's circle of friends. And – hadn't I felt it all along? – there was something synthetic about Dugald McBane: as if he had made up his own character but couldn't breathe life into it. . . .

To calm myself down I had a couple of drinks in a hotel bar in Sloane Square, in a thick atmosphere of well-heeled banality. Nobody in that bar appeared to have any problems that couldn't be solved by whisky and soda. I thought of Sally, and tried to do likewise. With the first I drank myself out of doing anything rash; with the second back into an even rasher mood. . . .

The Winslow Gardens Hotel, where Dugald lived, was one of those Kensingtonian mansions laboriously but incompletely converted into a semblance of a modern hotel. In the lounge were a number of old ladies digesting *Digests*, and I sat down and ordered coffee. In the shade of a potted palm, in the angle of the wall and a glass partition, I could command the reception desk unobtrusively. The day-porter was still on, and his attention was monopolized by ladies with white hair and guide-books. Keys jangled; an occasional breath of fresh air and youth came through the revolving door. But it was a long vigil and a nervous one. Finally I saw the night-porter arrive and take over.

I strolled up to the desk and said: 'Could you tell me if Mr McBane has come in? I was to have met him half an hour ago, but he may have missed me sitting in that corner.'

He turned and ran his finger along a row of hanging keys till he came to an empty hook marked 35. 'I'll just check, sir.' He plugged a lead into the house exchange and, with the receiver to his ear, smiled at two approaching ladies.

'Sorry, sir. Will you leave a message?'

'I could wait till he comes in.'

'Please yourself. But you may have to wait a long time . . . I hope you had a nice day, ladies?'

One said: 'My friend and I want to thank you for sending us to Kensington Palace. We wouldn't have missed it for worlds, would we, Bessie? Now we wonder if you could give us your name, so that we could send you a Christmas card from America.'

He beamed like a beefeater being photographed, and I decided that he was eminently corruptible. When my turn came again, I said: 'You must learn quite a lot about human nature from seeing guests slink to bed in the small hours. Do you notice what time people come in?'

I could have kicked myself for being so clumsy. He gave me a sharp look and said: 'Sometimes I do, sometimes I don't. But if I do, I reckon it's none of my business. . . . What name shall I give when the captain comes in?'

'Oh, don't bother,' I said. 'I'll ring him up later.'

I retreated with the remnants of my dignity. As I pushed one side of the revolving door to get out, somebody pushed the other to get in. We recognized each other midway. Now he was in and I was out. The same impulse made us both turn and push, and we were back again where we had started. He smiled faintly and shrugged his shoulders. He had a cigar in his mouth and he looked as though he had dined well. I stood my ground this time and the door decanted him with outstretched hand: 'Is the curse of sickness on this house or did you come to see me?'

'I was seeing a patient just round the corner and I just

dropped in on the off-chance. Where's Pat this evening?'

'In bed, worn out. Latta came to town this afternoon and Pat felt she had to hold his hand. It seems he feels guilty about the old woman's suicide, though I would have thought, from the point of view of all concerned, it was *just what the doctor ordered!*'

I thought this joke in doubtful taste.

'I don't think he'll feel guilty any more once he knows the true facts of the case.'

'The facts?'

'Yes, the facts. It wasn't suicide at all.'

I didn't see his expression as I said this. We were still standing by the revolving door, talking in low voices, and now he cast a quick glance behind him. I looked round too and saw the hall porter staring at us speculatively.

Dugald's hand on my elbow made me start: 'Let's go out and get a drink somewhere. This place is like a Sunday in Peeblesshire.'

Like all empire builders on leave in the Metropolis, Dugald was drawn irresistibly by the magic of Piccadilly Circus. In the corner of a lofty underground brasserie, where lack of heating and draughts added a touch of authentic Scandinavian starkness to the decorator's conception of a Meadhall, we settled down morosely beneath a moose's head and waited for strong drink to come. . . .

He shut one eye and stared with the other into his drink. Then he looked up suddenly over the rim of his glass.

'Has it ever occurred to you how many superfluous people have come into existence through one wee glass too many? There's a lot to be said for drug-addiction. . . . Well, cheerio! Here's to Mrs Van Dopp down in the shades!'

Chapter 10

The Shock of Recognition

'You see the point? If she had really intended to kill herself, she would hardly have bothered about asepsis.'

'Yes, I see.' Dugald frowned up over my head at the foolish face of the moose, then his eyes dropped and engaged mine. 'Do you think the police noticed that?'

'I don't think so, incredible though it may seem. It wasn't obvious without a very close inspection, and of course they knew from the porter about her relationship with Paul, which made suicide the most likely explanation. They also assumed from the state of the body that she had given herself a massive overdose. . . . '

'You mean you don't think she did have a massive overdose?' Dugald signed to the waiter and ordered two more double whiskies.

'Oh yes, I do, though one can't be certain till the autopsy results come through. But, calculating on the basis of her daily requirement and the amount of dope I handed out to her, I don't see how she managed it – she wouldn't have had enough left.'

He was pulling gently at his right ear. His colourless eyes had a curious look of latent bubbles that wouldn't come up to the surface. 'I suppose you couldn't have made a mistake about the strength of the stuff?'

The phrase 'just what the doctor ordered' came back to me. Was I being warned not to suspect him of a crime I could more easily have committed myself?

I said: 'I was very careful to warn her that the morphine was pure. She knew all about the dosage.'

'Then I don't see what you're getting at – unless you're trying to tell me that someone tampered with the bottle?'

My heart beat faster. I hadn't said anything about a bottle, and morphine in that form had been superseded, for individual use, by ampoules or soluble tablets. Now I thought I knew how the job could have been done.

His cigar was pointing straight at me. A blob of ash seemed to grow like a fungus from his lips. Was there really something unpleasant about the shape of his mouth, or was I imagining what I was looking for?

'Suppose you, for instance, had had the idea of giving the dope an extra kick – a kick that would land Mrs Van Dopp in Elysium? . . . Could you have managed it without her suspecting?'

'Yes, I think I could have. Guess how.'

A mere flicker of his facial muscles warned me that I was playing a dangerous game. I added quickly: 'But there's another possibility that just occurs to me. There was a half-empty glass of whisky on the bar in her room. If she had been drinking heavily before she gave herself the final shot, the alcohol might have weighed in with the depressant effect of the morphia. That way it could have been an accident. But we may never know. These reactions are very individual . . .'

The waiter came up to tell us we had time for one more before closing time.

'Well, here's to you and Pat'! I said. 'Things seem to be working out at last.'

Dugald said: 'I thought so, too. But this morning I had a cable from Kenya saying that my ranch had been attacked by Mau Mau. One of my cow boys was murdered and they went round the cattle compound with their pangas hacking the hamstrings of the Buraans. The capital loss is very serious, because of course I can't insure during the Emergency. I've got to get back out there as quickly as possible.'

I said: 'That's really tough. What are you going to do about Pat?'

'She's coming with me. We'll get married in Nairobi as soon as we've got things organized up at Bwala.'

I said: 'In view of her bad state of health, wouldn't it be better to get her out later?'

'I've done my best to stop her. But you know what she is – we've had all this out before.'

'But she'll be wanted to give evidence in the Rideout case. The police won't let her go.'

'If they want her, they can pay the journey to England. If they want her story they can have it sworn in Nairobi.'

I said: 'She's nervous and sleeping badly. As her friend and doctor, I can't approve of this.'

'Give her a good supply of drugs and she'll be all right. She seems neurotic, but she's a tough girl. It's over-civilization that makes neurotics; she'll be at home in the wilds, I'm telling you.'

A good supply of drugs. I remembered the portentous, stilted way Dugald had talked of Kenya at our first meeting. I felt sure he had intended to frighten her. But not – as Pat had thought – out of going to Kenya. He knew that she would go for the hell of it, however dangerous. He wanted to keep her on the edge, asthmatic, wavering between two worlds, between stimulating analeptics and sedative barbiturates that were likely to cause addiction. He had summed her up pretty shrewdly.

I said: 'Surely Pat won't want to leave the country without doing all she can for Mollie Rideout. She still believes Mollie innocent, doesn't she?'

'She would like to. But if the police think the brother did

it at Mollie's instigation, who are we, in our position, to interfere? You don't stick your neck out of the window if there's a man above you with a noose, waiting to hang somebody . . . '

Keep talking, Dugald. This is just what I wanted.

' . . . I learnt my lesson in the war, when my water-bottle was neatly holed by a sniper as I was giving a wounded Hun a drink. Sooner or later you've got to write off almost everybody in your life, because it's either them or you. . . . ' He looked up at the moose and added: 'And to the best of your knowledge, you're more use than they are!'

The lights were going off and on. As I got up to go, I took a good look at that moose. Its expression was no longer foolish, but sardonic. I said: 'I'd like to hear some time about your war experiences. But I suppose you hate discussing them?'

Dugald shivered irrelevantly. 'Let's go and get warm somewhere. I'm always frozen in this country. Shall we go to a Turkish bath?'

I dislike Turkish baths. The sight of so many rococo nudes, flaunting so much florid fatty tissue, blinds me to the undoubted merits of sweat-therapy and massage. The place was crowded with bodies, belonging mostly to middle-aged citizens worried about their weight and failing attractions. There were a few young men – of the bowler-hat-and-umbrella type, to judge from their voices and their haircuts – sweating out excesses of alcohol. But they all looked sadly wilted. Dugald stood out, in this hot-bed of thick flaccid plants, by the dynamism of his physical presence. Athletic, rather hairy, with considerable wound scars on his belly and thighs, he emerged from his clothes with obvious relish and led me through the more temperate and populous regions, walking lightly on the balls of his feet, his body tilted slightly forward. When we reached the hottest room, he spread his towel on the blistering duckboards that were supposed to prevent one being roasted by the tiled benches.

'This is more like it,' he said. 'The other rooms are a waste of time.'

He had a dragon tattooed on his right forearm, and as he glanced round at the other two heroes of the hot-room I had the impression that his personality was more forceful without clothes, almost aggressive. I couldn't help speculating about Pat's reaction to this formidable physique – the contrast it must have afforded with Latta's.

'I imagine you find Kenya hot enough for you – the political climate, anyway.'

He nodded. 'It's too bad they picked this moment to raid my ranch. They tried one night last year and got a rousing reception. I had put a dummy sitting with a gun across its knees and its back to the verandah window, as though waiting for an attack from the kitchen side of the house. I myself was sitting in the chicken house and I got two of them wriggling across the open ground to the verandah. Just like that . . . ' He clicked his tongue twice. He had a satisfied smile on his face, and it became fixed as his gaze rested on the young man sitting on the bench opposite.

I said: 'Your war experience seems to have stood you in good stead. What theatre did you serve in?'

'European. Mostly night work in coastal raids. That was Mau Mau stuff – knives and garottes. Those poor bloody Hun sentries!'

'I was just an M.O., patching up the damage you warriors did. But I can imagine there must have been a certain satisfaction in your sort of soldiering – stalking your man and getting him.'

'Satisfaction? The best thing about Commando work was feeling free to do the job in one's own way, cleanly, like an execution. I hate causing unnecessary suffering. Can't stand pain myself. . . . '

The young man opposite was now lying on his back with his knees drawn up and his eyes closed. Too young to have been in the war, I thought. I said: 'Did you find it difficult adjusting yourself after?'

Dugald was studying the tattoo mark on his arm, stroking it almost tenderly. 'I went to Kenya soon afterwards; I couldn't stand life in England: petty laws and restrictions: having to queue for everything: crowds. I loathe these London crowds. Since I've been home this time I've sometimes wondered if an atom bomb on London wouldn't solve the population problem.'

I let this pass and said: 'You must have been lonely out there without any women?'

'Oh, I jogged along. I was married, you know, when I first went to Bwala. My wife came from Connecticut. She was full of half-baked idealism about giving the natives their freedom, about the white man having no right to Kikuyu lands. She couldn't stand silence and she isolated herself from our few white neighbours by a lot of foolish anti-colonialist talk.'

'What makes you think Pat will do better? She's had enough of the Empire from Mrs Tatham, and once the novelty and excitement wear off . . . '

The young man sat up, tossed back golden hair from his eyes, and started massaging his chest.

'Pat's a wild girl, primitive. Have you ever seen her dancing with Latta?'

'Yes, but where's she going to dance at Bwala? With whom? Aren't you confusing primitive and decadent?'

'Don't worry so much, David. Pat and I know what we're doing.'

Conversation lapsed. The heat was difficult to bear. I closed my eyes, which were beginning to ache.

I am not an instinctive person. But if something hadn't impelled me to open my eyes at that precise moment I would have missed the sudden contraction of Dugald's eye-muscles; I would have missed the answering wink from the young man opposite, the hooding of a red, watery gleam that signalled recognition. Despite the heat my flesh crept. I knew now how Dugald had got along without women. That wink explained Pat's nervous state, her sudden turning towards me. But it didn't explain why she proposed to go to Kenya with Dugald. Was it possible she still didn't know?

I said: 'I'm going, Dugald, I can't stand this heat. By the way, when are you off?'

'Monday morning. I think I'll stay a bit longer, maybe sleep here.'

'By sea or air?'

'By air. There's no time to lose.'

I had to see Pat at once, while Dugald was well out of the way. I took the chance that she had remembered my advice about not unplugging her telephone at night. I was lucky.

'Okay,' she said, without enthusiasm. 'Make it in quarter of an hour and I'll come down and let you in. Though you *are* my doctor, one in the morning is hardly a suitable time to visit me, and we don't want to wake my mother or the servants with any more alarms, false or otherwise.'

'If anybody wakes you can say you were having palpitations . . . yes, palpitations, and a bubbly feeling in your legs.'

She was in fact looking very white, and this time the pallor wasn't artificial. But in her dressing-gown of faded green corduroy, with plain slippers of yellow velvet, she seemed to me more beautiful than ever. I was accustomed to consulting-room beauties unmasked in bed, too ill to bother what they looked like. Pat, unmasked, reminded me of Pat in the days before she started making up: she recovered her precarious virginity.

The heavy brocade lampshade cast a warm glow on the tossed-back sheets and on the brown fur of her worn teddybear – the one being in the world to whom she had never been in the slightest disloyal, except in changing its name from Treacle to Bromide.

'Do you mind if I get into bed again? Bring up the armchair so I can see you. And – oh, David, while you're at it, could you empty this ashtray into the wastepaper basket? I hate dirty ashtrays.'

'Because they make you feel guilty? You ought to feel guilty, smoking in bed.'

'I've only had one tonight. And I wouldn't have had that unless you'd rung me. I had to calm my nerves.' She lit another cigarette and, replacing the lighter on the bedside table, exhaled a mouthful of smoke under the lamp, watching it spiral up from the hot bulb. 'What's the matter now? You look cadaverous.'

'Washed out, mangled; in a Turkish bath. Pat, when you told me Dugald had puritan inhibitions about sleeping with you, was that what you really meant? ... It didn't strike you he might be queer?'

'It struck me he was – well, out of practice. If I thought he was queer would I be going to marry him? I'm a normal woman; you ought to know.'

'You might love him – I see that ... Oh, Pat, I'm so sorry, but it's my duty as your friend and doctor to tell you ... '

When I stopped speaking there was a long pause. Then Pat said:

'You were jealous from the beginning, weren't you?'

'I'm happily married and I want you to be too. I doubted if he was the man to make you happy. But now I see him in the context of all that's happened since, I'm not only worried about you, I'm desperately afraid.'

'Desperately afraid?' Pat lay back on the pillows and pulled the sheets up to her chin. She gazed at the lamplight on the ceiling. 'Why?'

'I don't understand what's going on. What, for instance, has changed your mind about Mollie Rideout? Dugald tells me you now think she's guilty.'

'Well, *someone* must have done it, and the police don't arrest people for nothing. Actually, I was suspicious of the Rideouts from the beginning, but I couldn't bear the way my mother took it for granted. I just thought she was trying to get at me.'

'It's true they have a case against the boy, that they may even succeed in getting him. They found the pipe that killed her in the hollow brass rod in her hanging-cupboard . . .'

'How do you know this, David?'

'I know it from Buxton, who lunched with me today. He said his men searched and found nothing at first. Why did he search again? He didn't say he'd had an anonymous call, but I think that's what happened. I went to see Mollie this evening. She's in a frightful state because she thinks she's been framed. And so do I. Two nights ago she had a mysterious visitor who said he was a journalist and so organized things that she had to go down to the aunt. The visitor, who wore a beard and had thick glasses, was observed by the pubkeeper opposite. He was nervous and he did this . . .' I pulled the lobe of my right ear.

Pat said coldly: 'Lots of people do that. Have you any better reason for suspecting Dugald?'

I said: 'I'll take the suspicious circumstances first – the way he picked you up on the boat; the dead set he made at your mother; his gentlemanly refusal to go to bed with you until he was ready for the operation; the fact that he left you early that morning after doping you with sleeping-pills. He did dope you that night, didn't he?'

Pat didn't answer. Her mouth had a strange obstinate twist that I had seen only once before, when she was accused of swimming naked in the river with a boy from the village school.

I went on relentlessly: 'Dugald has told me enough about his activities as a war-hero to make me certain that killing doesn't worry him. In fact he prides himself on doing it well.'

'That's a lie. He *was* a war-hero. And if you say he prides himself on doing it well, why didn't he kill Annie better? The poor soul was hit again and again. You didn't see her lying there, horribly mutilated.'

'All right, let's pass on. Did you know Mrs Van Dopp had been poisoned?'

'The papers say it was suicide. And so does Paul, now he's spoken to the pathologist; though at first he thought it must have been an accident. Anyway, who's side are you on, ours or Buxton's? . . . David!' – she stopped and looked at me with horror – 'I believe you asked that question because you hoped to trap me. Go on, get out of here before I ring for Cumberledge. *You're* the poisoner, you're trying to poison my mind against Dugald.'

I put out my hand and touched hers. She drew it away as if she had been stung. There were tears in her eyes, whether of rage or misery I couldn't tell. I said: 'Pat, sweetie, I'm not trying to trap you. I'm not trying to *poison* your mind against Dugald: I'm trying to rid it of a terrible illusion. I wouldn't be saying all this if I didn't really believe him to be a killer.'

'A killer.' She repeated the word as though she didn't understand what I was saying.

I said: 'Well, judge for yourself. I happen to know, and I've told Dugald, though the police still don't know, that Mrs Van Dopp was murdered. I won't go into my reasons now. The point is, who had a motive for killing her? – only you and Dugald and possibly me . . .'

'And Sally – what about Sally? Wasn't she worried about your career? Wasn't she once a hospital nurse?'

I shook my head: 'Sally and I are out, and I don't believe you could have done it even if you had wanted to. Dugald knows something about medicine. He also seems to know, without my telling him, that there was a *bottle* of morphine found beside Mrs Van Dopp's corpse. Morphine's unusual in that form nowadays. The stuff I used was old war stock I had saved from the army. You see?'

'I can't see that that proves anything. Couldn't he have seen it in the war himself? He was badly wounded twice and spent a lot of time in hospitals. So wouldn't he naturally visualize morphine in the same old bottles? – unless, of course, he were an addict himself, which he isn't.'

I said: 'You could be right about that, but you don't seem to see how it all adds up. Somehow I've got to make you face the fact that you've put your money on an outsider and lost it. . . . My God, what a fool I am – it's just struck me!'

'What has?' For the first time she looked really apprehensive.

'The telegram Dugald says he's had from Kenya, the sudden departure, the talk about a big capital loss. Have you invested any money in this ranch?'

' 'I haven't got a bean except my allowance. I'm supposed to be too irresponsible to have any money of my own.'

'But your mother's a rich woman, and Dugald's well in with her, far too well in. Do you know if she's been induced to part with any capital?'

'I've heard nothing about it. I know she's crazy about Dugald's ranch and plans to come to Kenya and visit us this spring. . . .'

'Have you any proof that this ranch exists?'

'Really, David, I'm not such a dupe as you want to make out. I've seen photos of the place, a whole book of photos – the house; the compound: Dugald with his horse, his dog, etc. . . . '

I smiled sceptically. But I felt I had impressed Pat at last and now I was ready to go.

'Anyway, think over what I've told you. I've one or two enquiries to make, and if they yield what I expect, I don't see how I can keep this thing from the police. Meanwhile, *be careful*. If he finds out that *you* suspect him . . . ' I kissed her on the forehead and went.

As I reached the door she called me back. 'David, come and sit down on my bed a minute.'

I sat down obediently, half ashamed of the power she still had over me. She was propped up against the pillows with her weight resting on her elbows. One shoulder strap had slipped off and that side of her nightdress was held up by the curve of her left breast. She said: 'I didn't mean that about your being jealous. I know you've always loved me, and sometimes I've even thought that if it hadn't been for Sally . . . ' Suddenly she put her arm on my shoulders, clasped her hand behind my neck and pulled me towards her.

I didn't resist. I followed her as far as I dared to begin with. I kissed her gently and she ran her lips along mine, moving her head slowly from side to side. But when she plunged her tongue into my mouth – tense, muscular, adept· – I wrenched myself away. 'No, Pat. No, no, no. I'm David – don't you remember me? – I'm not just anybody.'

She sighed and said: 'I just felt close to you, that's all. I often do and I wanted to be sure I hadn't driven you away. You're the one reliable person in my life.'

'My reliability, as far as you're concerned, depends on my remaining loyal to Sally.'

Pat smiled secretly and said nothing. I went on: 'I hate to

say this: but in the past, when you've shown signs of feeling close to me, it's been because you wanted to get something out of me! What is it this time?'

'I want your support, that's all. I'm in one hell of a jam and I'm utterly alone. That's the truth. Now please listen ...'

Chapter 11

A Whiff of *Ma Griffe*

I TIPTOED downstairs, not at all reassured by the relative noiselessness of my going. One feeble light was burning in the chandelier overhanging the stairway, giving out just enough radiance to attract the stares of putative Tatham ancestors hanging glumly round the walls. Their eyes seemed to follow me as I approached, disappearing one after another, as my shadow occulated them, into stolid expressionless faces.

I thought I remembered Pat switching off that light on the landing outside her bedroom.

As I rounded the bed, I saw another light below me. It was flooding across the carpeted hall, a bright inimical band that streaked a death-ray across my trajectory. I hesitated. Should I beat a retreat? The thought of Annie's murder decided me. I squared my shoulders and went on, with the heavy tread of a clear conscience.

I crossed the track of light and continued towards the front door. I was just putting on my overcoat, thinking I had got away with it, when a voice said: 'David, come in here.'

Mrs Tatham was wearing a dressing-gown of blue quilted silk. With her hair done for the night, set in spools of blue and silver thread, she looked forbidding, almost mythical. She was sitting at the end of the long Sheraton table with a glass of whisky and a decanter before her. One eyelid drooped, making that eye distinctly smaller than the other.

'What were you doing at this time of night, whispering with Pat in her bedroom?'

For a second I was the adolescent again, the little princess's whipping boy summoned to the presence of the Queen. Then I said:

'Why do you think I'm here? I'm a busy man who gets very little sleep and even less family life. Am I likely to be here on a social visit?'

'S'pose not. But all this secrecy, lights turned off, whispers? You've given me a terrible fright. What's the matter with her, eh?'

'She called me because she was having difficulty breathing; palpitations. I don't think she's in any condition to go to Kenya where she'll be remote from doctors and exposed to the worst psychological conditions. She needs rest . . .'

'Rot! She's done nothing but rest all her life. Dugald's the one I'm worried about. She's got to get out there and look after him. If she doesn't go now she may change her mind. She may take up again with that appalling young Latta, who's feeble-minded and not even English.'

'Would it matter so much if she changed her mind? I sometimes wonder if this Dugald, however desirable he seems to you, isn't dangerous for Pat. She's thirty now, she feels in a rut and she's ready to try anything to get out of it.'

'Too much of a man? Too strong, do you mean? If you weren't such a stick-in-the-mud, David, you'd want her to get out there and help fight those black devils. We're being driven back, driven back all over the Empire. And why? Because we're softened by socialism. A few men like Dugald are fighting our battles all over the world, and they're doing it with precious little support from home. If I were ten years younger I'd go out there and keep house for him myself, and I daresay, even now, I'd make him a better wife than Pat. I've got more guts.'

Mrs Tatham's change of life had been late and dramatic. I had been privileged to witness, as a kind of state secret, the diversion of her sexual drive, from individual to imperial ends. But sex was still there, a self-identification with the potent and aggressive males who manned the outposts of empire. I said cautiously: 'If you really want to help him, there are other ways you could do it. I gather he's lost most of his stock . . .'

'David, are you trying to teach me which side my bread's buttered? I believe in that boy and I'm behind him. I'm an old woman and a rich woman, and though Pat has never shown the slightest gratitude for all I've done for her, I'm prepared to give her one more chance. That chance is Dugald, and I'm going to see she doesn't squander it. I've been into the whole matter with Dugald and my lawyer and I've decided to sell the capital from which Pat draws her allowance and invest the proceeds in Dugald's ranch. If that won't make her stick to him, nothing will. But I want her out of the country before her relationship with that little trollop Mollie Rideout comes out in all the newspapers.'

I gasped. Pat, I knew, had about £800 a year: so that Dugald, at a rough estimate, was going to put his hands on £16,000.

'When does that investment take effect?'

'As soon as the capital can be realized. I don't want Pat running out at the last fence.'

Hans Crescent was as dark and quiet as the grave when I got in. So as not to wake Sally, I undressed in the bathroom and got into bed without turning on the light. I lay for a moment looking at the vague whiteness of her bed. Then it struck me that I couldn't hear her breathing. The bed was empty, unruffled.

I hadn't realized how jumpy I had been getting, both morally and physically. Suppose she had left? Suppose . . .

I ran down to the drawing-room and switched on the lights. She was lying on the sofa, fully dressed. She was twisted over on her side with her face buried in the cushions and one arm trailing behind her over the edge.

'Sally!' I said sharply. 'Sally!'

'What time is it? What's happened?' She sat up, rubbing her eyes. 'David, what on earth's the matter? You're as white as a sheet.' She was in my arms now and I was almost squeezing the life out of her.

'I thought ... God, you gave me a fright! Why didn't you go to bed?'

'How could I? I expected you hours ago.' She kissed me thoughtfully, then stiffened and pushed me away to the other end of the sofa. 'Well, have you proved the police wrong?'

She chain-smoked while I told her everything that had happened up to the time I left the Turkish bath. I paused there for her reactions. She got up and crouched in front of the fire, poking the embers abstractedly. At last she said: 'If you're right about this business in the Turkish bath, Pat must also know about it. And that means she must be involved with him in some crooked deal, or she wouldn't be going through the marriage and the journey to Kenya. I've always told you she would take to crime. Once lying and cheating the family becomes a habit, that's the next logical step. ... '

'She wouldn't necessarily know. I've had cases of *wives* who hadn't a clue as to what ailed their husbands.'

Sally dropped the poker and rounded on me. 'You've been with Pat again tonight. I knew it by your face as soon as I saw you. What's more, you stink of *ma griffe*, which you could hardly have put on in the Turkish bath! Why can't you be honest with me?'

'You didn't give me a chance to tell you. I had to go and warn her of the sort of person she's involved with.'

'And did she take the warning seriously?'

'I think she did, though she pretended not to believe me at

first. The fact is, she's in a hell of a jam. If Dugald is guilty of robbery and murder, she doesn't see how she can dissociate herself. He can't afford to let her out once she's turned against him. He'll say she was in the conspiracy.'

'If she's innocent, she can prove it.'

'Some hope! He's wangled capital out of Mrs Tatham to the tune of £16,000. It so happened that when Pat first met Dugald, she was badly in need of money. Still is. She owes various dressmakers £2000 and her allowance from Mrs Tatham is only £800 a year. In view of her bad relations with her mother and her previous attempts to defraud the old dragon, she wouldn't have a chance if this came out in court. Imagine Pat as a witness!'

Sally said: 'Exactly. Yet each new series of lies convinces you. Why should she be telling the truth now?'

I shrugged my shoulders. 'Because she's frightened, very frightened indeed. She feels isolated by all her lying.'

'Judging from the smell of *ma griffe*, she's not entirely isolated yet!'

'Sally, for heaven's sake, stop being jealous and bitter and get things straight. Out of common humanity, if not for the sake of the past, I can't abandon her to this man, *believing as I do that he intends to kill her*. Whatever she is, whatever she's done, I just can't.' I thought for a second, then I added: 'Do you think I'm such a bastard in my conscious mind as I apparently am in my subconscious one?'

'No-o. But I think you're just weak – so weak that you may destroy yourself as well as me in the effort to save Pat from herself. You've done all you can. I've done more than I can bear.'

I said: 'I could have been weaker. Look here, darling, if you'll see this thing through with me – and I can't possibly do it without your help – I promise you I'll never see Pat again. Is that a bargain?'

Sally looked at me oddly. 'Yes, you *do* love her, don't you? But how can we help her, short of going to the police, which would involve her in criminal proceedings?'

I said: 'I'll tell you tomorrow. I'm going to try and prove Dugald did it. And quickly.'

At lunchtime next morning, instead of coming home, I drove to the Cromwell Road and parked my car in a side street near Dugald's hotel. Then I went in and had a drink. As I had anticipated, there was a steady trickle of hotel guests through the hall, agglomerating at the reception desk: the day-porter was working hard dealing with luncheon dates and tourist enquiries. A page of about fourteen was handing out keys, messages and correspondence. I paid for my drink, and when the porter seemed suitably engaged in conversation, I strolled up to the desk and asked the page for the key to Room 35. He handed it over without looking twice at me.

I hadn't expected to find chambermaids on the floors at that hour and the whine of a vacuum cleaner coming through the door of room 34 made me hesitate, then duck into a lavatory nearly opposite. I waited there till the conclusive thud of the service door swinging to on the silence told me she had finished for the morning. Then I half opened the door of the lavatory and listened. Footsteps were muffled by the thick carpet, but voices were moving along the passage. A female one said: 'You must admit they were a bargain, Sydney?' To which a male voice grunted a cynical: 'Huh! I suppose the ballet tickets were a bargain too. . . . Bloody social racket!' I locked the door just in time to prevent the man coming in. I heard him breathing heavily on the other side of the keyhole; then he swore and went away down the passage.

A moment later I was in Dugald's room with the key in my pocket. I stood there for a moment looking at a photograph of an elderly woman with white hair drawn tightly back. Then my eye travelled to the wash basin. But there were no medicines, nothing on the glass shelf but shaving things, tooth things and a pile of used razor blades. In the sponge bag suspended from the towel rail there were some aspirins and a bottle of Alkaseltzer. The dressing-table was equally barren of what I was looking for: a bunch of keys, a stud-box containing medal ribbons, but no drugs, no false whiskers and no glasses. Next I tried the bedside table – void. Idly I picked up the book lying face downwards on the marble top. *Shadow over Kenya. A Settler's Diary of the Mau Mau Terror.* Flipping through the pages of the index, my eye was arrested by this entry: 'Capital Losses: through crop-burning, hamstringing of cattle, destruction of fences pp. 24–29: Author's Counter Measures pp. 30–32 . . . Ceremonies. Mau Mau recruits take secret oath . . .'

I sat down on the bed and started reading. I read three pages then put the book back in position.

So that was why Dugald's account of the oath-taking ceremony had sounded bookish, slightly phoney. He had quoted it almost verbatim.

Voices coming down the passage. I dived under the bed, pushing back a tin box to make room for myself. The voices went past, quarrelling, and I recognized them as the ones I had heard ten minutes before: their owners were on the way down to lunch. I came out dragging the box with me. But for the voices I wouldn't have thought of looking under the bed.

It was one of those strong black army boxes and it had Capt. D. G. McBane stencilled on it in white paint. It was locked. I got the bunch of keys off the dressing-table. Almost the first one I tried opened the box.

The contents was mostly army papers and correspondence,

and I picked up at random a bunch of letters tied up with blue ribbon. They were in cheap envelopes, all postmarked Kilmarnock, Ayrshire, addressed by the failing hand of an elderly woman. The top one, which I opened first, had been written in Kilmarnock Hospital during the war. It ended like this: *My darling boy, if the operation fails, I shan't mind going because I'm so proud of all you've done for the country. I always knew you would make good in the end. God bless you. Mother.'*

I looked at the photograph of the woman with the grey hair, then I put the letter back in its envelope and picked another from the bottom of the pile. I soon saw the significance of the large plain envelope on which was written FROM MOTHER '37–38. They were letters to a convict in some London prison. But I could find no reference to the crime.

I left the door key on the outside of the door, hoping the chambermaid would notice it when she came back from lunch and take it straight down to the reception desk. I didn't want to risk a confrontation with the hall porter.

As I was starting up my car, a man came out of a little coffee-shop opposite and walked away in the direction of the hotel. There was something familiar about his gait and build, and since the street was empty I started up and reversed rapidly in pursuit of him. He heard me coming and quickened his step, and as I drew level he stopped and turned his back, peering with keen interest into the window of a small dressmaker. The hooting of a taxi told me I was blocking the street; but I drove away tolerably satisfied that he was the man who had followed me out of the pub in Chelsea.

I decided to say nothing about this to Sally. I didn't want to hear: 'I told you to keep out of this'. But somehow I had to deal with a persistent and aggressive mental microbe that had been wangling its poison into my ego ever since the lunch with Buxton. I stopped at a telephone booth on the way home and rang up Scotland Yard. Buxton was out, but they gave me the number he had left and finally the master's voice came through, amplified by alcohol. It emanated from the Wildman Club, where he was lunching with the Carthusian stockbroker.

'Mortimer, you must be psychic! Or did you feel your ears burning?'

I said: 'I'm developing my extra-sensory perceptions. But meanwhile I'd be intrigued to know more about that journalist fellow who had a private session with Mollie Rideout in the interval between your first search and the finding of the weapon. Was he genuine?'

'First I've heard about any such man,' he said. 'But it sounds as if you may be on to something important. Could you give me the details?'

I gave him the details briefly, adding: 'But I understood from Mollie that she had told you this. Even if she didn't, I feel you must have known all about it, with your watchdog in the pub opposite.'

'My watchdog?'

'Yes, I was followed last night. And the same dogfaced sleuth is on the job again today.'

Buxton laughed, as only a member of the Wildman can after a lunch of steak and kidney pudding washed down with Ploughman's Dark Special. 'You really must be imagining things, old boy. Maybe you've got a suspicious wife or something. Look here, if he bothers you again, just step up and ask him if he's aware that he's committing an indictable nuisance!'

I rang off, baffled.

Sally was waiting for me, nibbling Gruyère nervously: and while she was getting lunch I followed her round, giving her the story between sips of beer. Even if Buxton *was* using me as a pawn, I had solid reason to be pleased with myself, both as a man of action and a thinker. A plan was forming in my mind.

She said: 'I suppose your case against Dugald is still mainly based on presumption – not enough material proof for the police. But what you've found out this morning strengthens it enormously: I believe you're right. You know, I've been thinking this morning. All sorts of wild ideas have been through my head, but this one keeps recurring: couldn't you give Pat some infection or dope that would torpedo the Kenya scheme for some months?'

'I've thought of that myself and discarded it. Nothing physical would do, not even force. In a way I've already given her a shot – a shot of reality, which is the only antidote to Dugald. I'll give her the follow-up at the psychological moment. By which time she should be feeling the reaction sufficiently strongly to decide against flying to Kenya on Monday. But even that's not a cure. The only cure is for her to find out about him for herself. I think she'll be impressed by his behaviour once he knows her suspicions are aroused. I want to observe that behaviour too. It may be vital for the Rideouts as well as for Pat. And I want to observe it under lab conditions . . .'

'Lab conditions?' – Sally looked at my glass, to be sure I was only drinking beer.

'At the cottage, away from London, friends and work. Just the four of us in the middle of the Sussex woods, with our mutual suspicions about sex and crime. Pat's not going to let herself be convinced about Dugald until she gets it from Dugald himself. She's no physical coward . . .'

'But, darling, you can't be serious. You said yourself he may try to kill her!'

'Not until he's certain the game's up. Anyway, we'll be there, ready for any emergency.'

'Explain.'

I explained. Her comment was: 'That's all very fine – a setting for a bad thriller. In real life things don't work out so neatly. To begin with, I don't suppose for a moment they'll come to us for their last weekend. They've got packing to do, and, anyway, why should they want to spend it with us?'

'I think Pat will want to, in these circumstances. And if Pat does, so will Dugald. His plan is to be concerned about her health until the time's ripe for it to take a marked turn for the worse.'

Sally said: 'Are you trying to make my flesh creep? Or has something come over you – a sort of madness?'

A sudden loneliness made me stretch out my hand and take Sally's: 'The situation's mad, not I. Couldn't you try coming into it, instead of looking on from the outside?'

Chapter 12

A Voice cried: 'Sleep No More!'

I HAD planned it very carefully. Dugald was to have had the bedroom next to ours. So that when he went to Pat's room – I assumed they would want to talk as far away from us as possible – he would have to go down four steps that creaked like gallows-chains in a wind. Behind the oak headboard of Pat's bed a hired microphone was to have been hidden, with a long flex leading under the carpeting to my office tape-recorder in our bedroom. I was to have gone down early on Friday to fix up my laboratory. Arrangements had been made for a medical substitute.

That was the sole item that went according to plan.

The invitation 'tickled' Pat 'to death': 'What's the snag, Sally? Have you invited Buxton for the weekend too? Or has David suddenly decided to acquit my fiancé of all his imaginary crimes?'

Sally's reply – I had it from her own lips afterwards – was thoroughly characteristic: 'David's suspicions seem to be mainly emotional in origin. I think he feels they've gone beyond the facts and he wants to make amends before it's too late to save his relationship with you!' Pat's rejoinder, if accurately reported, was equally characteristic: 'Jealous men are heaven! So long as they don't have firearms!'

Dugald's reply to our invitation isn't recorded beyond mere acceptance. But he must have thought it over and decided that there was something fishy. Everything had been fixed: Llewellyn had been sent shopping and telephoning;

124

my suitcase was already stowed in the boot of my car; when Mrs Tatham came through the telephone wire like the wrong end of a running fuse: 'What's this, David? You're proposing to remove *my* family from *me* for their last weekend in England? Isn't this rather thoughtless, or is it just modern? Well, I certainly can't let them go. But I don't see why you two shouldn't join us at Maiden ... Pat wants you ... No, no *demurrage*, if that's the right word ... You'll be much more comfortable, and Dugald might be lucky enough to see the last of my saffron crocuses in bloom ... even the Astors can't grow them at Cliveden ... '

There was nothing for it but to obey. Mrs Tatham had begotten the marriage settlement that fulfilled Dugald's criminal project; my plan had to be adapted. Though the chances of success were gravely diminished, I had at least one advantage over fate. I had known Maiden Manor from childhood: I knew almost every corner of the house as only children can know the rooms and passages they have played in. But there was no longer any question of creaking steps and microphones. Cumberledge and the maids would be there ahead of me: Mrs Tatham would arrange where we all slept: she would chaperone Pat as closely as Argus chaperoned Io.

Sally had never been to Maiden Manor. My father had retired from the living some years before my marriage: and Mrs Tatham, despite my position as the family doctor in London, had never thought fit to invite me until now, when the invitation was forced from her.

'That must be the church,' Sally said, 'over there in the elms with the sun glinting on the weathercock. ... Did you really shoot at it with a .22 rifle?'

The car swerved as I rubbed my behind. 'That's an episode I don't wish to be reminded of.'

We turned into the lodge gates, and now the church disengaged itself from the trees. 'I want to see the rectory,' Sally said. 'Is that it beyond the red brick wall?'

'No, but you can see it clearly from the manor house ...'
I nearly added: 'You can see it so distinctly that Pat and I used to signal to each other from our bedroom windows.' But I knew what Sally was thinking and I wanted to avoid giving the impression that the place still seemed romantic.

We swung round the last bend of the drive. 'There it is,' I said. 'Not bad at first sight, considering it's all George Fifth Tudor? The worst are those tall clusters of red-brick chimneys and those frightful diamond-paned windows. But you'll like the garden. A lot of that is very old and it needs a house that sticks out in surprising places.'

Sally saw Pat's Sunbeam at the door and looked nervously at her watch: 'Pat and Dugald seem to be there already. Oh, Lord, and there's Cumberledge standing in the porch. She did say twelve-thirty, didn't she?'

'That means they've telephoned up from the lodge. Now, darling, if you're going to suffer from social nerves you won't get through this particular weekend party. You must save your nerves for other things!'

Sally dabbed powder on her face and mumbled: 'I can deal with murderers, even rivals in love. But that Mrs Tatham scares me!'

'Madam is with her Ladyship and the Captain in the garden. She said to show you up to your room and tell you lunch is at one.'

I wrested our suitcase from Cumberledge. It didn't seem right that a man like that should have to make physical efforts.

'Don't bother to take us up. Just tell us which room. I know the house as well as you do.'

'The blue room, sir, if you remember.'

126

'Is that the one next door to her ladyship's, overlooking the shrubbery?'

'No, sir, the other side, over the dining-room.'

'That's Mrs Tatham's room at the end of that passage – the one with the door open. Isn't that Chinese four-poster just perfect for her? Imagine anybody else being able to sleep surrounded by orange dragons swarming up poles! . . . Wait here a moment. I've got an idea.' I left Sally with the suit-case in the main passage and opened the door of the room next to Mrs Tatham's.

'I knew it. She's put Dugald in there, about a quarter of a mile away from Pat. You know, I think she's really jealous of Pat, as well as being used to Pat's nocturnal visits to men's bedrooms.'

We found them in the garden, and Mrs Tatham led us into the drawing-room. We sat round in warm sunlight on the chintz-covered seats of the big bay-window: and presently cocktails were brought. The first cocktail produced a feeling of euphoria. Mrs Tatham had a smoker's cough. Dugald gravely told a story about a man whose friends told him that if he didn't stop smoking he would end up by coughing up his guts. One night, when he was drunk, his friends gutted a rabbit and put the entrails in his bed. In the morning he came down pale and shaken, and his friends said: 'You look ghastly. Did the worst happen?' 'Yes,' he said, 'but with the help of God and a toothbrush I managed to get them back again!'

This wasn't the sort of story that Mrs Tatham normally appreciated. But Dugald appealed to the coarse side of her and made her feel liberated. There was a latent hysteria in the gathering. We all laughed heartily.

The second cocktail was one too many. Pat burnt a hole in her slacks, and Mrs Tatham took the opportunity to observe, most unjustly, that Pat looked decadent in slacks. I rushed to her defence. Sally supported me: 'I agree. I wear them too and I've got an enormous behind.' Dugald said: 'If men with bellies can wear kilts, women with arses can wear slacks: and that's the back and front of it.'

'Dugald,' said Mrs Tatham indulgently. 'You're not in darkest Africa yet. I didn't realize you were so coarse.'

In one way I was glad that we were beginning to get on one another's nerves. At lunch Pat looked sulky and withdrawn. She hardly touched her food, and of course Mrs Tatham had to draw attention to it:

'You'll have a better appetite leading a healthier life in Africa. But you won't have Mrs Cumberledge to cook for you.'

'She'll have better food than this,' said Dugald rudely. 'You think you live well, you upper crust people in this island, but I guarantee my black cook can knock spots off Mrs Cumberledge. She can . . . '

'Ssh!' Pat interrupted him, casting a quick glance at Cumberledge who was hovering inscrutably round the side-board. 'Everybody in this room understands English, and some a great deal better than you do.'

'Don't jump on Dugald like that,' said Mrs Tatham. 'Sally doesn't jump on David, do you, my dear?' This was almost the first remark she had addressed to Sally, and the best Sally could do was to pass the buck: 'Do I jump on you, David?'

I said feebly: 'If you did, I should be ironed out flat.' We were always joking about this sort of thing, but I realized from the look she gave me that I shouldn't have said it. The wound was still wide open.

After lunch I got Pat alone for a minute on the lawn, while Mrs Tatham was showing Sally and Dugald her saffrons.

'Have you thought over all I told you?'

She nodded, and I said: 'You haven't said anything to him yet?... Good, then, don't. By the way, did you realize he had been in prison?'

'Lots of people have been in prison. Does that make them murderers, or what?'

'I couldn't say. I don't know why he went to prison. But I wouldn't be too happy about the £16,000 your mother is settling on him, as the price of getting you fixed for life.'

She said a very rude word, softly and thoughtfully. The others were coming back across the lawn. I patted her head and said: 'Keep that under your mop too.' By the way she was tapping her foot on the ground I felt certain she had decided to have it out with him. I didn't need to say any more.

'Well, now,' said Mrs Tatham benignly, – there was no doubt that Dugald had a softening effect on her – 'what are you young things going to do? Personally, I'm going up to have a rest.'

Dugald said: 'I'd like to stretch my legs. Coming for a walk, Patricia?'

Pat said 'Yes,' unexpectedly. She never walked a step if she could help it. I said pointedly: 'Why don't you go too, darling? I ought to write some letters.'

We had agreed to do everything we could to prevent Pat and Dugald being alone together in the daytime. At night I was solely responsible for what might happen...

While they were out I visited Pat's room. It had been done up and reorganized. The window with the little leaded balcony on which Pat had torn her underclothes climbing out to take a rain shower-bath had now been filled with ordinary panes. In front of it, in place of the chintz-draped dressing table I remembered, now stood the heavy Gothic linen-chest where she had kept her dolls and their trousseaux. The chest had been moved from its old position to make room for a built-in hanging-cupboard, which occupied the whole wall. These were not the only changes I noted. But I had come to reconnoitre, not to dream . . .

I was having a nap when Sally got back from her walk. 'That's the first time I've ever been for a walk with a murderer – or with an ex-convict for that matter.'

'How did it feel?'

'Creepy. He turns out to share my passion for wild flowers. You wouldn't have suspected him of that, would you?'

'That's the feminine streak, no doubt. Do you remember Charlie Chaplin as Monsieur Verdoux? He loved flowers and women . . . and money. Surely the thing about most murderers is that they dissociate themselves from their crimes. Most of the time they're just ordinary people among ordinary people. Dr Jekyll on holiday from Mr Hyde.'

Sally sighed and said darkly: 'What we do doesn't represent what we are! That's the most comforting of the classic bedtime thoughts.'

Tea brought us all together again. Looking at Pat sitting on the pouffe before the fire, in a tight pink sweater designed to clash subtly with her hair, I related her to the little girl whose hair was always tied back with green ribbon; whose gestures and expressions, even at the age of ten, suggested sexual maturity. Suddenly I was overwhelmed by the pressure of associations. I got up and parted the heavy brocade curtains. The pale sun was setting on clipped hedges half in shadow, and the liquescence of the dewy grass beyond led my eye in a flash to the rectory a quarter of a mile away. Lights sprang up in it as I watched, and the familiar silhouette seemed to darken round my mental picture of my father sitting down in his study with a cup of tea, to start work on his Sunday sermon . . .

'Living in the past, David?'

I turned round to find Pat just behind me, looking over my shoulder. Beyond her was the group round the fire. Mrs Tatham was showing Dugald photographs of horses she had once ridden to hounds. Sally was knitting her thoughts into a sweater. I let the curtains fall together with a feeling of hopelessness. Pat's eyes were sparkling and her toes tapping. 'Let's have the gramophone,' she said. 'This tea session always gets me down.' She started flipping through a pile of records.

Mrs Tatham said: 'Can't we be quiet for a minute, Pat? *Must* you turn that thing on?'

'I feel restless. I want to *do* something.'

'What about that tapestry I bought you? I can't imagine how you're going to pass the evenings in Kenya!'

Pat said: 'It'll be more exciting there, I imagine . . . ' Suddenly she swung round on her hips and put out her tongue at Mrs Tatham. '*I shall be waiting to be assassinated.*'

There was an awful silence. Both Dugald and Sally looked up quickly and a muscle flickered in Dugald's cheek. Mrs Tatham blew her nose and rang the bell. It was left to Sally, overcome by nerves, to break the thin ice with a veritable pile-driver of tact:

'*I wouldn't be scared of the Mau Mau, if I were married to a man like Dugald.*'

Only music, loud music, could drown the echoes of that terrible *double-entendre* . . .

After dinner we played vingt-et-un and gin rummy. Then Pat proposed dancing. Nobody except Pat really wanted to dance. But I stuck to my policy of backing her up. Hadn't she said she was alone and miserable? And hadn't I promised Sally that I wouldn't see her again after this weekend?

Pat seemed to sense my romantic crisis, and when we were dancing I half enjoyed the way she clung to me, though I knew it was making Sally furious. I was a buoy, bobbing in the dark, rough sea of her emotions. I felt she wanted to believe I was fast anchored to the rock, that I guaranteed her against herself; yet couldn't resist hoping she would be powerful enough to snap the cable.

'Do you remember the last time we danced?' I asked. 'By the way, how is Paul making out?'

'Oh, he's all right. Or will be when he gets used to his freedom. I told him we were down here for the weekend and he said he might come over sometime, just to say "goodbye and to hell with you". Dickie's apparently so pleased with him that he's going to give him a contract. That'll be one man off my conscience.'

I said: 'If he comes, that'll really make the party go! I shouldn't imagine he's Dugald's cup of tea. And I happen to know he isn't your mother's.'

'Dugald's got to swallow that cup, or else . . . Mother will just sweep up to bed, withering Paul with a Siberian "Good night, Mr Latta, and goodbye!" '

More drinks came in. Wine had followed the cocktails, and brandy the wine. The White Horse galloped behind. Mrs Tatham had induced Dugald to dance, and now she was repairing her face while Dugald walked round with Sally. In that huge room with no band and only two couples, dancing was a kind of emotional drift. We wandered into corners, talking. We stopped at intervals to swallow some whisky or look at a picture. Pat and I had drifted into an alcove near the door when she said very quietly: 'I can't stand this room with so few people and everybody watching everybody else. Let's go down to *our place* – do you remember?'

I remembered only too well. I hesitated, then I said: 'All right, but I'd better ask Sally first or she'll inevitably think the worst – who wouldn't?'

'Oh come on! She and Dugald are talking earnestly about giant Hellebores on the Mountains of the Moon. You can't believe how well they got on this afternoon. If she shares your views about him, she certainly shows no signs of being repelled.'

I said: 'That's exactly what she says about you, when you're with him. My conclusion is that really dangerous and perverted men have a special fascination for women.'

'Well, you told me not to let him suspect anything . . . *they're both looking at us now . . . Come on, let's get away and talk.*'

'Our place' was under the main stairs. It had been transformed into an air-raid shelter during the war, and now I hardly recognized it, with a sofa and deckchairs and a camp-bed.

Pat closed the door and led me by the hand to the sofa. Then she got up and switched off the light. Now she was close to me, really close, closer than if we had been actually touching. She said: 'You wanted to come, didn't you? You thought of it before me? You wanted to escape with me and be as we were before life closed in on us.'

I sighed an admission then wrenched myself back from the edge of the precipice: 'As far as I was concerned, it was always precarious, always happiness mixed with miserable apprehension. And now here I am again, feeling almost unbearably guilty.'

'But so do I! That's just what I mean. Isn't it wonderful to feel so guilty? At any moment we may be taken in adultery. Sally will divorce you and Dugald'll slit your throat from ear to ear . . . ' She sighed.

I said: 'It shows how different we really are; that you still find this sort of situation funny.'

'I know it isn't funny really. But I'm canned as a whelk and frankly I don't care.'

'Ssh!' I said. 'Talk in a whisper. *You* may be canned, but I'm NOT.'

The muffled explosion of that 'not' was followed by a nervous silence. Pat jumped when I brushed away a cobweb that stirred against my forehead in the draught between the door and the ventilator. 'What's wrong, darling? Have you got a headache?' I felt the chill of her ring against my forehead, then her fingers combing up through my hair. 'I always loved that calf's lick of yours. Annie used to say it was a sign of character. I should have acted like Delilah and cut it off, then you wouldn't have had any character.'

'Pat,' I whispered fiercely, 'what *is* all this comedy in aid of? There's no magic in deliberately escaping.'

'Isn't there? Are you quite sure?'

'Quite sure. You always enjoyed making me do things I didn't really want to do. But I'm not playing any more. And I'm not going to be played with – do you understand?' I was suddenly furious. 'Do you understand, you destructive bitch . . . '

'Stop it, you fool, you're hurting my wrist. Let go of me or I'll scream and tear my dress.'

I let go and fumbled for cigarettes. I lit one and handed it to her as an olive-branch: in the flare of the match I had seen that she was trembling. I said: 'I was thinking principally of Sally, but I was also thinking of myself being tortured.'

There was another silence. The distant throb of the bass continuum from the radiogram grew louder. I knew that somebody had opened the drawing-room door.

'Stop being divided, then,' Pat said. 'Stop asking to be tortured. Go on, Big Brother, back to your happy bourgeois marriage! *Just one chaste goodbye kiss* . . . '

We moved apart, blinking. A brilliant wedge of light had been driven between us, and Sally stood in the middle of it, pale as death. I remember noticing her bare arms hanging down listlessly. On the left arm the vaccination pits were filled with shadow, like three black nailheads in her flesh . . .

'Come on, David, it's time to go to bed.'

Sally went straight to the wash-basin and started to do her teeth viciously. I tried to explain to the frothing face in the mirror. When she had finished she spat, wiped her mouth and said: 'It's no use explaining. In lab work it's results that count. It's obvious you only got me here to cover up your affair with Pat. Dugald's a godsend, why don't you face it?'

'You seem to think so, anyway, murderer or no murderer.'

'Beggars can't be choosers. Nor, in certain circumstances, can buggers. My position here is so frightful; I've got to save my face as best I can. Actually I feel rather close to Dugald. Murderers understand one another.'

'*What did you say?*'

Sally smiled to herself and slipped her dress over her head. She took off her brassière and pants, walked over to the long mirror and stood contemplating her naked body. She spoke softly to her reflection:

'Poor, dull, solid Sally, wife to Doctor Mortimer! Such a worthy, controlled, responsible girl, with good values and intellectual interests – they all said David was so lucky!'

I said: 'Sally, darling, what's happened to you?' I moved towards her, but she said: 'Keep right away. If you want a woman, you've got your whore close by.' She swung round and picked up her nightdress, and walked heavily over to the bed.

'Sally,' I insisted, 'what's happened? What did you mean just now when you said "murderers understand one another"?'

She got into bed and lit a cigarette. She was perfectly calm as she said: 'I killed Mrs Van Dopp. But I did it for you, not for Pat and Dugald. I did it because I loved you and I thought she was out to ruin your career.'

I studied her face. The grey, intelligent eyes conveyed no hint of mental disturbance. The slight upwardness of the corners of her mouth suggested cool interest in my reactions.

I said warily: 'How did you do it?'

'Oh, it was quite easy, child's play really. Do you remember me asking, when you had told me what she was after, how many grains she was having daily?'

'Yes, I do.'

'Well, afterwards – it must have been Sunday afternoon, when you were out – I got out your big toxicology book and looked up the relative lethal doses. I knew you were going to use your private store of morphine because the narcotics man hasn't got that listed. I knew you would start with the half-empty bottle, and I guessed you would give her another to go on with. That was the one that interested me.'

'But there are five bottles in my secret store. How did you know which one I would use?'

'I made certain you would use the one I wanted by pushing the other three behind it on the shelf.'

'I see. And then?'

'Then I went to the official narcotics cupboard and got out six whole grain tablets. I took a hypodermic, sucked up the contents of the bottle through the rubber cap and dissolved the tablets in the solution. Then I squirted it back and put the syringe away again. It was only a question of days before she came round to the doctored bottle. She might have tolerated even that dose – who can tell? – if she hadn't been drinking at the same time.'

I said: 'So far, so good. But I shan't believe a word of this till I've counted the tablets in the official cupboard.'

'Oh, I shouldn't bother to do that. Just take a look at the

narcotics book – you'll find an entry neatly forged in your handwriting.'

What does a man say when his wife admits murdering to save his career? – 'You're wonderful, darling?'

No, not if he happens to be a doctor who had taken an oath to preserve human life.

'I won't tell you what I think of what you've done; I shall have to ponder that. What concerns me at the moment is why in God's name you had to tell me about it?'

'I had to tell you to save you from worse than a blackmailer, from an evil unscrupulous woman.'

'And how, pray, is this going to save me from her?'

We had fallen into an icy formality of speech.

Sally hesitated, drew at her cigarette, then stubbed it out coolly in the ashtray, grinding it till the last wisp of smoke stopped rising.

'You've got to stop persecuting Dugald. I want Pat to marry him and go to Kenya. We're together again, David, working for our own marriage, not against theirs. If you do anything more to try and convict Dugald, I shall go and confess my crime to the police. What's more, I shall make you my accomplice; just what Pat thinks Dugald would do to her. In the circumstances I would be believed, surely . . . No, don't look at me with such horror. It's time you learned that wives are serious about being wives. Good night.'

I switched off the light and lay back with my eyes shut, seeing Sally's face staring through my darkness.

Chapter 13

Laboratory Conditions?

THE rift between Sally and me seemed to deepen the space between our beds till it became uncrossable. From the ground floor an arabesque of trumpet music was suddenly superimposed on the beat of swing: a bar or two, archaic, plangent, then nothing but the monotonous thumping. A moment later I heard a door slam at the other end of the house and I guessed Mrs Tatham had come up to bed. That left Pat alone with Dugald. Suppose she chose that moment to precipitate the crisis.

Just one chaste goodbye kiss.

As if in answer to my question, the thumping of percussion suddenly stopped. A car droned along the main road from Taplow. It could have been coming up the drive, it sounded so near. Yet it was as remote as a star swinging noiselessly through time.

I couldn't bear the things I was imagining.

'Sally!' I whispered.

I spoke her name louder and was rewarded with a cold, 'What?'

'This is one of those nights when a good sleep might do us good.'

'I thought I heard a voice cry "Sleep no more!"'

'That's melodrama. I'm going to take some barbiturate. Do you want some too?'

'What's the use? We've got to face ourselves and what I've done.'

'Let's not face anything till the morning.' I got out of bed and gave her three capsules with a glass of water. When she touched my hand in the dark, a little shiver ran through me, though the room wasn't a bit cold.

I shook two capsules into my own hand, put it up to my mouth and swallowed. I gulped down the rest of the water.

But the capsules went back into the bottle.

Quarter of an hour later Sally was out for the count. I bent over her and listened to her breathing. Then I dressed quickly and slipped out.

There was a light showing through the keyhole in Mrs Tatham's room as I passed the end of her passage. I pictured her sitting at her dressing-table, twisting and pinning her hair, patting and moulding the old flesh with absorbed Byzantine artifice.

The drawing-room door was shut. I could hear Pat and Dugald talking, but I couldn't distinguish a single word. The fireplace was half-way down the same wall of that huge room and I guessed they were sitting on the sofa with their backs turned to me.

That gave me the nerve to open the door. I turned the handle very slowly, pulling it towards me until it would turn no more. Then I exerted a slight forward pressure. It opened without a sound, and as I gently released the handle I heard Pat laugh: 'Now you're being stuffy – I was only trying to make you jealous, to see how you'd react. And I must say your reactions disappoint me. You should have seen Sally's face when she found us in there! Anybody would have thought she'd found us in bed together: I really felt sorry for David, being hauled upstairs by the short hairs . . . '

'Why did you want to see how I reacted?' Dugald's voice was measured and unamused.

'Because I'm fed up with all this restraint. Nowadays that gives a woman pause . . . '

'We've had all this out countless times. I thought you finally understood how I felt about this. If I hadn't kept up the moral façade, your mother might have smelt a rat.'

'But why keep it up in private? Or have you come to believe you're really such a gentleman? I sometimes wonder if you're not trying to put the squeeze on me ...'

After a pause Dugald said: 'I don't know exactly what you mean by that, but I'm going to put the squeeze on you now!'

There was no more talk for a long time – one of the longest and most unpleasant I remember. And it didn't help to tell myself that I was getting my deserts for eavesdropping.

Eventually Pat said: 'Am I dreaming, or are you really such a voluptuous monster? I can't believe it's you, Dugald.' She was so palpably insincere that I wasn't at all surprised to hear him say: 'David could do better, eh?'

Just behind me in the passage there was a French window leading into the garden. Suddenly the curtains over it billowed out; the drawing-room chimney sucked up the draught, and the door opened, checked with a thud by a rubber stopper.

Dugald said: 'What the hell was that?' From the loudness of his voice I gathered that he had turned round and was staring at the doorway. I shrank back in time to hear him add: 'I thought it was someone coming in.'

Pat said: 'There's a wind getting up. Let's go to my room. If we go by the back stairs my mother won't hear anything ...'

I didn't wait to hear any more. Fortunately I was in my socks and my flight was silent, by ordinary peacetime English standards. I went up the front stairs, a slight short-cut to Pat's bedroom. My only thought was: 'I can't abandon her now.'

I got there the length of the house ahead of them. The curtains were drawn and I fumbled in pitch darkness for the catch of the built-in hanging cupboard. I couldn't find it.

Then I remembered the big linen-chest in the window. I had once hidden there playing Sardines and if I had had time to stop and think, I would have realized that I had grown out of it. As it was, I think I was attracted to that unpromising piece of furniture, so associated with my childhood and half amorous games. It occurs to me now, though this may seem far-fetched, that the chest also had Freudian associations. The very word 'chest', linked with Pat and her unpredictable bronchi, was an emotional as well as a medical symbol. That might explain why I didn't choose the obvious hiding-place, behind the curtains. Had I done that things would have turned out differently. . . .

I lowered the lid over myself only a few seconds before the bedroom light went on and I heard Dugald say to Pat:

'There *was* someone listening outside the door. I heard footsteps running ahead of us.'

Pat said: 'Your trouble is you've got Mau Mau on the brain. You imagine stealthy figures in the night. Either you've got a persecution complex, or . . . '

'Or what?'

Springs creaked; a match was struck; pillows were patted. I could see nothing but the keyhole of the chest – an elongated 8 made of light. There were vague streaks of luminosity where the lid didn't fit. I imagined Pat elongated on the bed, and Dugald sitting on it, studying her, waiting . . .

Finally Pat said in a husky voice: 'Will you get me an ephedrine pill and a glass of water? – you'll find them in the medicine cupboard in the bathroom.'

Creaking of springs: footsteps, then the chink of bottles. Six feet away from me a drawer was quietly opened and shut. I knew it was the drawer of the bedside table because Pat didn't move off the bed. When Dugald came back my heart was thumping so loudly it seemed that the noise must carry right through the house, as the beat of the jazz band had done.

Pat said: 'Thank you. Now will you draw the curtains and open the window. This heating dries up the air so that I can't breathe.'

Central heating. If she hadn't mentioned it, I probably wouldn't have guessed that there was a radiator behind the chest. Now I realized how stifling it was. I put out my hand cautiously and found that the wood was hot.

Curtain-rings clicked and a second later the faint light through my keyhole was cut off as Dugald leant over my hiding-place to get at the window. The sash squeaked to its limit with a bang and I heard a gust of wind come sighing through the open window. But he must have opened it at the top: I felt no draught, no breath of freshness.

Pat was saying: 'No, one's enough: David said so. He thinks I'm getting too drug-minded, and that if I'm not careful I may go into a tailspin.'

Dugald said: 'To hell with that old woman, David! As I told you on Wednesday night, you'll be as right as rain once we're out of this bloody country, away from the life you've been leading. You'll be a new girl when you've got something to think of besides yourself. New scenery, new people, adventure, work.'

'David may be an old woman, but he's an old friend too, and he happens to be my doctor. He thinks I ought to wait at least a couple of months and then come out and join you.'

'That's not what he was saying a few days ago. What's going on, Patricia?'

'What do you mean, "what's going on?" I don't much like that tone of voice.'

'What's made him change his mind so suddenly? What's made you change yours? When I got the cable from Kenya,

142

you said nothing on earth would stop you coming with me.'

'I'm feeling lousy, that's all. Well, not quite all . . . I'm not so happy about *us* any more . . . '

'I see . . . uh-huh.' There was cold wariness in his voice. Springs creaked and I pictured him shifting his position, his brain secretly mobilizing a highly trained muscular system.

'Suppose my mother backed out of this investment deal? Would you still want to marry me?'

Silence, except for the surflike noise of wind in distant trees. I shifted my head, straining to listen, afraid I might miss something they said. I had cramp now, but I didn't dare do anything about it. They were still mute, presumably staring at each other – two pairs of eyes like surgical probes held steadily in gloved faces.

Dugald said: 'The money has got nothing to do with it – no more than it ever had, that is. We were agreed from the beginning that your mother had more money than she knew what to do with, and that was part of the romance, planning a way to make her part with it in a good cause. We were in this together. We still are, unless . . . ' There was a gesture here, a facial expression – something that didn't work with Pat.

'Okay, then, I put you up to it, we were in it together. But as far as I was concerned it was always romance first, business second: and there was no connexion between the two except that the second made the first more practicable. But with you it was the other way round, wasn't it? The romance was subsidiary to the business . . . *if there ever was any romance* . . . '

I moved one hand cautiously downwards and tried massaging my thigh, digging hard into the twitching muscle with thumb and forefinger. Dugald must have turned round, listening. Pat said: 'Oh, it's only that old chest: it always creaks at night.'

Dugald seemed dissatisfied. I held my breath till he spoke

again: 'Now what put this queer idea into your head?'

'Last night I had a ghastly dream about you. I dreamt I came to visit you in prison. We talked through a kind of hatch with bars. You were surprised but not a bit pleased to see me because you didn't know I knew you were there. But I didn't know *why* you were there, and when I asked you, you just laughed in my face and said: "Then you're a bigger fool than I thought!" Suddenly there were no bars between us. I felt your hands round my neck trying to strangle me . . . it was horrible, horrible . . .'

I was just thinking: 'God, what an actress!' when Dugald's voice rapped like knuckles on my wooden shelter: 'Cut out the dreams. Cut out the act. You're like me, a realist. Who told you I had been in prison?'

'Nobody told me. I dreamt it, I tell you. I don't dream very often, but when I do my dreams are apt to haunt me . . .'

There was a sharp crack, and then a small muffled voice saying:

'Is that supposed to help matters?'

'That was just to wake you out of your dream. Come on, now: who told you I had been in prison – the doctor?'

Silence, punctuated by savage slaps. I counted five, then I couldn't stand it any longer. I shifted my position painfully, trying to roll over on my front, so that I could straighten up and take the weight of the lid on my shoulders. I had an idea that I could spring up suddenly and get at him before he had the chance to recover from his surprise at seeing me. But my legs had gone to sleep. I was too noisy and too slow. My shoulders barely raised the lid before a crushing weight forced me down again. As I collapsed back into the blackness, hitting my head against the edge of the chest, I heard Dugald's voice saying: 'Settle down, Medic. We're going to have a little talk – you and Pat and I.'

'David! Oh you fool, you interfering fool!'

'*Interfering fool!* – a likely story! So that's what you two were planning under the stairs; and now we've identified the eavesdropper, too. Of all the filthy tricks . . . '

'I swear I didn't know David was there. Ask him.'

Sweat stung my eyes, so that I didn't feel the blood trickling into them as I struggled to get myself back into a bearable position. I didn't even know I had hit my head.

I banged on the wood with my fists. 'Let me out of here, or I'll shout for help . . . ' My voice died away and I heard myself panting like an animal in a trap. There was a harsh squeak as the key turned in the lock and I relaxed for a moment, exhausted, crushed.

'You've made your bed, Medic, and you can bloody well lie on it. You're under lock and key, and if you shout or bang again on that chest, I'll give Pat the beating she deserves, do you hear me?'

As my physical strength came back my mind faced a black wave of horror that made me want to struggle, kick, scream – anything to get out, to breathe and stretch. The wave had almost overwhelmed me when the word 'claustrophobia' shot up like a danger-signal into my consciousness, so that I became *aware* of what was happening to me. With a great effort I managed to control my breathing, and gradually the psychological tumult subsided. It was the cool menace of Dugald's voice that had stopped me panicking. I could still be of use, I told myself, if I could control my fear and listen. Pat was alone in the room with a murderer . . .

Dugald was sitting on the chest, swinging his legs. His heels rattled against the wood, sending little impulses of pain through my aching, congested head.

Suddenly I heard Pat say: 'Get off that chest and let David out.'

Dugald laughed unconvincingly. 'Really, Patricia, you

shouldn't take your dreams so seriously. You wouldn't dare use that thing.'

'Get off that chest and unlock it. I don't want to shoot you. But if you make me do it, David will say it was self-defence.'

The heels gave a final rap, and Dugald slid off the chest. The key turned, this way and that: he seemed to be having difficulty. Then light came through the keyhole, so that I could see the mark on my black trousers where a splinter had torn into my knee, unnoticed among all the other aches and pains. I pushed against the lid with all my strength.

But it was still locked.

'There you are,' Dugald was saying, 'would you like me to go down and get it?'

Pat said: 'I'm afraid you'll have to stay there a bit longer, David. He's thrown the key out of the window. Sit down again, Dugald. No, on the chest. I don't want you to come any nearer.'

Chapter 14

Effects of Poisoning a Mind

As his weight settled on the chest again, he uttered a long sigh that could have expressed astonishment or resignation.

'All right. I'm sorry I lost my temper.' His voice sounded relaxed, but the drumming of his heels conveyed the strain he was under. 'Be fair to me, Pat. What does a man do when he finds that his woman has been double-crossing him? He's got a right to lose his temper, hasn't he?'

'It depends on the way he loses it. And I'm not "your woman" any longer. This is where we part company.'

For a second I thought she intended to shoot him, and the same thought must have struck Dugald. His heels stopped drumming abruptly.

'Now be reasonable, Pat. Put that gun away in the drawer, or else I'll have to come and get it. I can't talk while I'm being threatened.'

'You'll "get it" all right, if you do come! I've found out, just in time, what you're really like. When you hit me, you lost all your power over me. I'm a free woman now. I'm so free I could even kill you if necessary. But there's one more thing I'd really like to know before I go and telephone to the police. *Did you kill your first wife?*'

'Pat, you're raving, hysterical. You think you hate me, don't you? But really you love me. It's just that this bastard, snooping doctor has been steadily poisoning your mind. Now be a honey and put that gun away, or I shall really have to come and take it from you . . .'

I hardly followed the rest of the conversation. Pat brought up everything I had told her about him, and more. It was clear that she had loved him, against her better judgement; and now she hated him with all the fury of wounded feminine pride. What essentially mattered was that she, a beautiful and unhappy woman, frustrated all these years by her inability to reciprocate a man's love, had finally given herself body and soul to a pervert, and to a pervert who was using her to get money, who would discard her as soon as he could.

Dugald soon gave up answering her. I don't think he was even listening. He merely concentrated on telling her, over and over again, to put away the gun in the drawer. He must have said: 'Or I'll come and take it' at least ten times, in the same monotonous low voice, before it dawned on me that he was using a deliberate technique, that Pat was being gradually hypnotized. I noticed that her voice was sinking, her aggressiveness diminishing. I had an idea that he was staring at her steadily, making her words boomerang . . .

Suddenly the chest creaked loudly. I knew that he was standing up.

'You don't really believe all this second-hand slander, and now you're losing confidence in yourself. Look at the way your hand's shaking. For the last time, *put that gun away in the drawer* . . . '

'Come one step nearer and I'll shoot you. I mean it. I mean it. Oh, I mean . . . '

The last word, if she uttered it, was drowned by the shot, a ghost of a shot, as though the bullet had a defective cap. The second shot was so much louder that the sound of Dugald's body falling seemed to follow logically.

There was the little thud of the revolver falling on the carpet; a quick light succession of footfalls; then the more precise thump she made as she fell on her knees beside the body.

'Oh, God, oh, God, what have I done?' She was sobbing out endearments, and I had to beat on the chest and shout her name before she realized who I was and whence the sound came. She had completely forgotten me.

'I think he's dead, David.' She was calm again. 'But there may still be a chance.'

'Take your mirror and hold it to his lips ... Nothing? Not a trace of clouding? ... Well, then, listen carefully and do exactly as I tell you ...'

I could hear doors opening, far away; voices. 'Lock the door,' I said. 'Quick!'

Shocked into childish obedience, she repeated the story after me. 'He had been beating me ... he wanted to kill me ... I found the gun, loaded, in his coat pocket ... I was so frightened I didn't know what I was doing ...'

'Press his fingers on the butt of the revolver ... all right? Now run down and get that key.'

I shall never forget Mrs Tatham's cry when she saw Dugald lying dead on the floor: 'My boy, my son! She was never any good, she was never my daughter. And now she's killed you and run away ... What's that? Who's hiding in there?' It was extraordinary how she managed to switch off her grief and turn on the querulous anger, 'Come out, I say. Come out at once!'

'It's David. Dugald locked me in here and threw the key out of the window ... He would have murdered Pat if she hadn't shot him ... she's gone down to get the key.'

Mrs Tatham didn't understand. 'Come out, you coward. Do something, for God's sake, *do* something.' She rattled desperately at the lid of the chest. 'Ah, Cumberledge, quick! Get a hammer and chisel ... No, what's the use? Go and telephone Doctor Smithers.'

'You'll do nothing of the sort!' It was Buxton's voice, hard and authoritative. 'Telephone the Bucks County Police and ask for a police officer and the divisional surgeon. Who has the key to this chest?'

'I don't know,' said Mrs Tatham faintly: and then, rallying somewhat: 'And what are *you* doing in my house at this time of night, giving orders to my servants?'

'I came to question Mr McBane and your foster-daughter in connection with the Ovington Square murder. I seem to have come too late ...'

At that moment Pat arrived with the key. But it was Buxton who turned it in the lock and stood stonily meeting my dazed blinks as I climbed out, battered and dishevelled, and stumbling.

'Mortimer again! – ' he couldn't resist that whisper of malice – 'always in at the death!' He raised his voice to add kindly: 'Well, I knew you were here, and I think I can guess roughly what you were doing. Sit down, there's a good chap, while I take a preliminary look at McBane. Could I have that lamp from the bedside table?'

Dugald was lying on his back, staring up at us with half-closed eyes. The corners of his mouth turned down a little, as though registering disappointment at the way his plans had gone wrong. I couldn't see any sign of the wound. But in the angle between his side and his outstretched arm, the white carpet was slowly turning crimson.

Pat didn't look at him. She stood outside the circle of the lamplight, aloof and quite motionless, as though rematerialized in a strange new world after the agony and wrench of disembodiment.

Buxton grunted and rose to his feet.

'Now, young lady, tell me exactly what happened,' He picked up the revolver, sniffed the barrel, broke it open.

She repeated my lesson almost word for word, while Buxton listened impassively. Her performance was all the more impressive to me because of the toneless, automatic voice. But Buxton didn't look impressed. He began to question her, bluntly, almost brutally.

And then, most opportunely, she fainted. With Buxton's assistance I lifted her up and put her head between her knees. She was still wearing the low black evening sweater she had put on for dinner, with a full skirt of purple silk; and now her rich brandy-coloured hair cascaded down into the gleaming silk valley, bringing out the bloodless pallor of her neck and cheeks in a haunting pre-Raphaelite colour-scheme. As my hands rested on her white shoulders, something made me look up at Buxton. He was observing me closely, and the shadow between his eyebrows suggested that he was in two minds about something . . .

She stirred and sat up, staring at Dugald with huge eyes. Then she covered them with her hand and started to shake her head. Buxton signed to Mrs Tatham, who was sitting bolt upright on a hard chair, blowing out her lips and fanning herself like a dowager overcome at a servants' ball.

'Perhaps you would take your daughter downstairs and give her some brandy. But no drugs – is that understood? I want her clear in the head. I shall have more questions to put to her later.'

He shut the door after them and turned to me with a serious face.

'Murderer or no murderer – and I have reasons to believe that McBane may have been the man I wanted – I have to keep remembering that dead men tell no tales, but that live ones do – even the best of them – when their emotions are involved. Eh, Mortimer? Have a look at him.'

I unbuttoned Dugald's waistcoat and shirt, pulling them up under his arms, so that his face was covered. There was no mark on the firm hairy body but the scars I had noticed in the Turkish bath.

'Now turn him over. I'll help you . . . heave-ho . . . Now, what do you make of that?'

I pulled up the blood-soaked shirt till I found the wound, still frothing, just below and to the right of the left shoulder-blade. I wiped the blood away with the tail of his shirt. The edges of the small, neat wound were bluish.

'The entry wound,' I said, and got up to wash my hands.

'You see what I mean? If Lady Killaloe's story is correct and she really shot him in self-defence, why did she shoot him in the back? I'm afraid this is going to take a great deal of explaining away – in view of the fact that she had already risked a prison sentence for covering him up in the Ovington Square business. And your position in this affair will have to be made less ambiguous . . .'

I was stunned by this development. *Come one step nearer, Dugald, and I'll shoot . . . David will witness it was in self-defence . . . free to kill you if necessary . . .* Yet she had shot him in the back. Why, why? Unless by shooting him she had intended to conceal the extent of our own involvement in his crimes. Who, but I, knew she had conspired to cheat her mother? . . . Surely she wasn't still counting on me?

I had to gain time to think things out.

I said: 'How did you come to know all this?'

'I suspected it the first day I met Lady Killaloe. My suspicions were increased by Nellie Bligh, who told me Lady Killaloe had sent her sister out against her will and against Mrs. Tatham's express instructions.'

'The cheat, the rotten old cheat!'

'But what could I do against the alibi you insisted on giving her? I felt sure you wouldn't have stuck to your guns so long unless you really believed her to be in danger. And even then you were only prepared to do it because you were very, very fond of her . . . Oh yes, Nellie Bligh told me that too.'

'When I gave her the alibi I didn't realize she had been in her mother's house. She told me she had been with McBane at a friend's flat and that she was afraid of the Press getting hold of the story. Her decree nisi might have gone up in smoke, you see. I thought I was giving her a purely sexual alibi; and by the time I realized she had lied to me the consequences of telling the truth would have been serious. But what made you so sure it was an alibi?'

'The night Mrs Van Dopp committed suicide she rang up and told me about Latta's telephone call to Ovington Square. It seems that she hated Lady Killaloe: she thought she was responsible for young Latta leaving her. Young Latta was also pretty keen on the girl. That's why he kept his mouth shut when I interviewed him.'

I thought of Sally sleeping heavily in our bedroom and Mrs Van Dopp, disembowelled, in her refrigerator. I said: 'But if you knew for certain it was an alibi, why didn't you do something about it?'

'Because I still had nothing positive against McBane. I only knew that he *could* have committed the murder. But I did have something positive against Syd Rideout – so positive that it stank, but it was a nice tit-bit to throw to the public. By that time I had seen enough of you, Mortimer, to be convinced that your conscience was uneasy. I knew your background was solid, the best in England . . . '

'Oh hell!' I interrupted. 'You can't be serious.'

'Never been more serious in my life. I knew my best chance of getting *inside* the case was to make you think that you alone stood between the real murderer and a gross miscarriage of justice. Without you knowing it, I made you an honorary member of the Force, and meanwhile I had your comings and goings observed. From the moment you left me after our lunch at the Wildman – oh yes, that lunch was carefully planned – one of three men was always on your tail. We knew that Mollie Rideout's visitor was phoney, though we couldn't get any line on him. We just had to hope that you, with your special knowledge of the Ovington Square circle, would eventually lead us to him. We gathered from the barmaid at the Coldstream that you thought you were on a breast-high scent. And when you searched McBane's hotel-room, we closed in behind you and gave the hall-porter a bit more than McBane had given him. What interested us particularly were the air-tickets to Nairobi; they were for tomorrow's flight. That made it all rather urgent, though I couldn't even question him until I had found out more about his background . . . '

'Stop a minute,' I said. 'Where did you find the air-tickets?'

'In his pigeon-hole at the Reception desk. We didn't open the letter, of course. We just rang up BOAC . . . '

'Did you find out that he had a criminal record?'

'He had a record as a homosexual, if you call that criminal, which I don't as between consenting adults. That's why he was discharged from the army before the end of the war. Pity, really, such a warrior, so warped. But that information, you see, made his relationship with this girl extremely suspect.'

We both stood for a moment looking down at Dugald. Then I said: 'I knew about that too and I told Lady Killaloe. That was why she decided to break with him on the eve of their departure to Kenya. She also knew, because I told her, that he had got Mrs Tatham to invest £16,000 in this bogus ranch of his . . . Oh yes, it was bogus.'

Buxton shook his head. 'I checked on that and it was perfectly genuine. His first wife bought it for him, but when she left she got most of her capital out. She's married again now and lives in New England.'

'Oh, well!' I was beginning to feel worse than deflated, guilty. I couldn't meet the dead stare of Dugald's eyes. 'Anyway, Lady Killaloe herself had begun to suspect he had murdered Annie Bligh, and she feared she might be next on the list. In the absence of any material proof, there was nothing for it but to get the truth out of him. I knew she would challenge him very soon. That's why I planned this weekend: that's why I was hiding in the chest, without her knowledge, of course.'

'Would she get the truth out of him by shooting him in the back? Oh come, Doctor! I appreciate your loyalty to her, but I must warn you she's facing a charge of murder. Why, if she really thought her life was threatened, didn't she contact the police? Why? – unless she risked exposure as an accessory in the theft of her mother's jewels?'

The wind in the elms sounded like waves breaking. A rush of damp air came through the open window, making the sashes rattle ominously. I got up and stood looking out into the darkness, seeing the countryside as I knew it by daylight. I saw the outline of a tall yew hedge grow sharp and blacken as the gleam of approaching headlights momentarily caught it. Then another puff of wind gently buffeted me. It was like the breath of inspiration, making my vision shorten and dwell on the balcony outside, on the balustrade roped and knotted with the thick muscular limbs of a wistaria that shone white in the radiance from the room behind me, on either side of my shadow. I turned abruptly and went to sit on the bed, while my eye roved round the room searching . . .

Buxton was saying: 'She must have fired that shot with a cool mind and a steady hand; and – what's more – she must have kept the gun hidden till the right moment. If he had seen her pointing it at him, he would hardly have turned his back would he? . . . Do you still confirm the story she told?'

'In every detail but one, which now strikes me as being of immense significance. I heard *two* shots.'

'Then there must have been an echo, possibly reflected from those big trees out there. She only fired once.' He tossed the revolver on to the bed. 'See for yourself.'

I didn't look at the revolver, I had just seen something else. Just out of the line between the head of the bed and the chest was the armchair into which I had flopped on emerging from my hiding-place. It was covered in apple-green chintz with a pattern of yellow Florentine roses. And right in the middle of a cluster of roses, where my head must have rested while I was sitting there, was a black mark like a stain. I got up and examined it, then I said: 'If she only fired once, then she didn't shoot him. Come and have a look at this.'

He went straight to the wall behind the chair and put his finger into a hole in the plaster. Then, clicking his tongue, he turned and gazed out of the window.

'By God, I believe you're right: that's what comes of talking. He must have climbed up the creeper. Quick – do you see the rain on the window? – if there are any footprints, they'll soon disappear.'

On the way down we met a uniformed police sergeant and a doctor hurrying slowly in the wake of the stately Cumberledge. Buxton paused on the stairs to give brief instructions, then dashed on down into the hall.

'You know the grounds? How do we get round to that window?' He seized a torch lying on the hall table. As we came through the front door, the police ambulance drew up. There were three cars now. Lights were blazing all over the house.

It was raining hard by the time we turned the angle of the house. The lawn I remembered below Pat's window had now been replaced by crazy paving and the wistaria grew out of a flower bed. Buxton bent down and pushed a clump of stocks aside, thrusting the torch near the earth. He rummaged for a moment, then switched his attention to an adjacent rose bush, from which he presently rose, swearing volubly and sucking a scratch on the back of his hand. The torch beam rose slowly up the thick, writhing trunk of the wistaria. Steely rods of rain slanted across the light.

'Hold this torch, will you. I'm going to try and get on the creeper without stepping on the flower bed.'

He tried three times, and by the third try the clump of stocks was battered to the ground. He shouted up to the window: 'Sergeant, come out on the balcony, will you?'

A face peered down at us, blinking. Raindrops glistened on a toothbrush moustache.

'Have you a torch? ... Right, examine the balcony floor, especially to the left of the window, and tell me if you can see any footprints.'

'Sorry, Sir. Can't see a thing.'

'Then he must have taken his shoes off to climb, otherwise the dew would have ... Oh, blast this bloody rain! Look here, Mortimer, he can't be far away. He must have heard me arrive and avoided the drive ... I've a good mind to ...'

No doubt he had a good mind to alert the police of three counties and cordon off the roads for miles round. But at that moment we heard a car coming up the drive.

We were sheltering in the porch by the time it drew up. Paul Latta, immaculate in tails, stepped delicately out and ran across the gravel to join us with his head buried between hunched shoulders.

'Hulloa there!' he greeted me. 'There seems to be quite a party going on. Pat told me to turn up any time before one, and here I am! I've made it with just three minutes to spare.' Then he saw Buxton standing there and said, 'Wow! This means trouble! How are you going on, Inspector?' He giggled nervously, and I smelt liquor on his breath.

Buxton said: 'There's serious trouble in this house, and you'd better go away, young man, before you get involved in it . . . No, on second thoughts, you can stay if you behave yourself. Go and join Lady Killaloe in the drawing-room.' He turned to me and added: 'Better go with him, Mortimer. I want the whole bunch of you together. Now where's the telephone in this house?'

Chapter 15

'Must You be so Brutal, Inspector?'

MRS TATHAM had gone to bed. Pat lay full length on the drawing-room sofa, chain-smoking and soliloquizing. Paul sat on the floor beside her, absorbing her every word and movement as she rambled on, trying to talk herself out of an attack of nervous exhaustion. 'I don't believe I could have pulled the trigger,' she was saying, 'if he hadn't sprung forward like that... But what's the use of thinking things otherwise?... It was better for him to be shot by me then and there than have to go through all those months of imprisonment and trial and sentence... No, I can't say I'm really sorry. I had to kill that side of myself...'

As she talked on, her hand moved up and down her face, feeling the places where Dugald had hurt her. Paul's eyes hardly left her face. His long legs stretched towards the fire and the glistening patent-leather shoes twitched to the rhythm of some jazz tune he was humming under his breath. I noticed how big and masculine his feet were, in contrast to the tapering, feminine hands with their beautifully manicured nails. Pat hardly seemed aware of his presence. I don't think she was very aware of mine either until I managed to get through on the right wavelength:

'Go on blaming yourself, if you like. But the truth of it is that the bullet you fired missed him completely.'

Her cigarette fell from her hand and she scrabbled listlessly down the back of the sofa. Eventually she found it, and said:

'If you're trying to say that Dugald died of heart-failure, you're wasting your bedside talk on me.'

'It isn't bedside talk. He was shot from behind by somebody hiding out on the balcony, somebody who was watching and listening, who expected to find you alone . . .'

Paul drew up his legs suddenly. But before doing so he had the reflex to pull up his trousers and preserve the crease. In the white gap between the top of his socks and the fall of his trousers there was a long, fresh double scratch.

I felt absurdly elated by this discovery and I found myself looking at Paul in quite a new way, as a personality to be reckoned with. It now seemed to me that his melancholy southern eyes were less passive and empty than I had thought. There was something about the face too – the very weakness of the mouth and jaw suggested strictly lawless potentialities; and this, I now realized, had been very well captured by the surrealist portrait in Mrs van Dopp's chaotic living-room. I tilted my head very slightly, almost unconsciously trying to recapture the particular effect of the picture's askewness. Paul saw me looking at him and smiled a weak, self-conscious smile, smoothing back his hair with long fingers.

'But who could possibly have wanted to kill Dugald?' Pat seemed to be making a great effort to rise above her feelings. Such an effort, in fact, that anybody who didn't know her might well have wondered if she had any feelings at all.

'I don't know. An accomplice? Perhaps somebody that loved you? Whoever it was, it looks as if he was trying to save your life.'

I had committed the error of making Paul self-conscious. He caught the direction of an involuntary glance and got up rather suddenly, letting his trousers fall back over his ankles. I added: 'As a matter of fact, Pat, he did you a double good turn. If he hadn't fired before you, and made you miss, you would have been suspected of shooting Dugald for reasons other than self-defence.'

'What other reasons?'

'You might have been suspected of getting rid of an accomplice. Buxton came here to question you *both* about the Ovington Square murder. He had found out almost as much as I had about Dugald, including the fact that he was a known homo, and that, of course, made him postulate a different relationship between you – a partnership in the jewel-theft. You see, he knew you were in the house that night.'

Pat said: 'For Christ's sake someone give me another drink.'

Paul jumped to it and poured her a brandy and soda, and she added, without thanking him: 'Let Buxton suspect me of anything he wants to – I'm beyond caring.'

I said: 'If you take that defeatist attitude, you're going to get into serious trouble. You've got to wake up, now, and tell the *truth* – that you knew nothing whatever *about Dugald's financial dealings with your mother*, until I informed you about them.' I reinforced this important point with a frown, which she acknowledged with a barely perceptible nod. 'And incidentally,' I pursued. 'you owe it to Sally and me to come through this as clean as you can. Buxton will be back in a moment to question you, and now that Dugald's dead and unindictable, we don't want to be sucked into criminal proceedings just because you don't care about yourself. You've got to think of Paul, too. He lied gallantly for you at a moment when he must have been sorely tempted to tell the truth and let you stew in your own juice. That's the least you can do for him, to show your appreciation of the good turn he did you.'

'Of the good turn, not of *me*!' Paul said with surprising acidity. 'She's never appreciated anything about me but my turns and my dancing and other performances. I was so fed up with her at the time that for two pins I would have told *all*. But not to *that* nark! I wouldn't have given *him* the satisfaction . . .'

Paul drew himself up. His chest swelled. His eyes seemed to start from his head. Finger and thumb came together under his nose, caressing the imaginary stubble. His voice hardened and his accent became more masculine as he said: 'You're Latta – Mr Paul Latta, eh? . . . Now I understand that on Friday night you agreed to act as Lady Killaloe's escort to the opening of a new – ahem, bottle-club, right? . . . Now try and remember clearly – when did she change her mind? . . . Ah, so you weren't aware that she had made another engagement? . . . ' He broke down, giggling at his own cleverness, and Pat said: 'Oh, shut up, Paul. This isn't a moment to try and be funny.'

I said: 'He was only trying to cheer us up. You must agree he does Buxton to the life.' But I was thinking: 'Long legs, Pat's physical type; Dugald had long legs too; he must have been about the same height.'

Pat said: 'What I want to know is, how did Buxton find out for certain that we were in my mother's house that night?'

I looked hard at Paul as I said: 'Mrs van Dopp told him. She rang up the night she committed suicide. I must say, I was staggered when Buxton told me that. If she was really in such despair about your leaving her I shouldn't have thought she would have bothered to do that last mean act. She did kill herself because of you, didn't she?'

'The police say so, but I just can't believe it. We had a bit of a set-to when I told her to lay off blackmail, or else . . . But by the time I actually left she was as calm as a cucumber. She *told* me that dope was all that mattered now in her life. She said: ' — off and do what you like, but don't think I'm going to have you back." '

'You mean you don't think she did kill herself?'

'Nope. I think it was an accident. Once, when she was loaded, she said to me: "Look, love, if I ever take an overdose, don't forget the milk of paradise: and if that fails, get me pumped out pretty bloody quick." '

It was extraordinary. Mrs Van Dopp might have been in the room. Pat shivered and said: 'Paul! Haven't you any decency at all?'

That phrase struck me. I was still trying to catch up with my own ideas, which were being revolutionized too quickly. Now I felt I had taken a jump forward. . . .

The door opened, startling us all. It was Buxton, hot and wet and angry. He stood in front of the fire and steamed. Obviously he had found nothing.

As he filled his pipe he glared at each of us in turn, as though wondering who to pick on. Finally he picked on Pat, and he was in no mood to spare her feelings.

'Now that McBane's dead, you've no reason to shield him any longer. And I may say that your own future may depend on the accuracy of your answers to my questions. Now cast your mind back to last Friday night. You left the Mortimers at twelve. What did you do after that?'

Pat was telling the truth. I was sure of that because her story so closely resembled the one she had told me in the Knightsbridge bar. The sex part obviously embarrassed Buxton, and he felt inclined to let her gloss over that. But it was important for Pat to get it across that she had had no suspicion of Dugald's homosexuality, and I chipped in once or twice to refresh her memory – to Buxton's visible irritation.

She was describing her nervous state after the unsuccessful love-making, when I happened to notice Paul's face. It was working with passion. And the passion – I couldn't doubt it – was hate.

I don't know how long the questioning went on. I can only judge, from memory of Pat's exhaustion slowly turning into truculence, that it was almost morning when I made my dramatic intervention. I surprised myself as well as the others. I hadn't realized how far it is possible for the subconscious mind to go on working on a problem while the conscious mind is otherwise engaged.

'Has it occurred to you,' I said, 'that the jewel theft could have been committed *afterwards*, to camouflage the real motive of the crime?'

Buxton, in the middle of lighting his third pipe, stopped sucking and swivelled round on the stool from which he had been bombarding the exhausted Pat.

'Of course it occurred to me. Will you please stop interrupting?' The flaring match burnt his fingers and he tossed it angrily into the fire. He licked his fingers and said: 'On second thoughts, I might as well hear what's on your mind. You've been inside this from the beginning, and you have certain advantages over me.'

I said: 'This has just occurred to me. Look at it this way. At least five people, plus their contacts, must have thought the house was empty that night. *But only one person could possibly have known that McBane and Lady Killaloe were there.* Suppose that person had been Lady Killaloe's lover, and now found himself not only supplanted, but spurned. That person knew from his experience as her lover that Friday was Annie's night out. He still had the latchkey to the house, because she hadn't had the face to ask for it back. Let's say he is a neurotic with a passionate nature. He is apparently good-natured and superficial; insults don't appear to penetrate him any more than water penetrates a duck's back. But he remembers insults and stores them up, and one day he decides to be revenged on the woman who has hurt him so much. Friday night is ideal for this revenge, because there is a chance that McBane will swing for it. He goes to Ovington Square and hides in the shrubbery in the gardens, watching for McBane to come out. He knows her intimate habits, you see: he knows she can't actually *sleep* with anybody; soon she will be alone. . . . Some time after two he sees the door open. McBane hurries away round the corner. He climbs the fence, let's himself into the silent house, and creeps up the stairs. Maybe he intends to strangle her in her sleep, guessing that she will have taken sleeping tablets. He has reached the landing outside the door when suddenly he hears a noise – Annie has heard him coming up the steps and she has thrown open her window to look out and see who it is. But he doesn't know Annie is there. He thinks Lady Killaloe is still awake and he decides to retreat back to the hall and bide his time. But then he hears Lady Killaloe – as he thinks – coming down after him. He goes down still further, to the basement. The footsteps are still following, and he hides in the glory-hole. Then the lights go on and he seizes up the lead piping . . . '

'No, no, Paul. NO!' I saw the look on Pat's face and misinterpreted it. But Buxton had been watching Paul Latta and kicked his wrist up a second before he fired, so that the shot went over Pat's head, shattering the bulb of the standard lamp behind the sofa.

The fire had gone out, and for a moment all was darkness except for the steady glow of Pat's cigarette. There was a sound of scuffling and panting. Then a sharp, animal scream, succeeded by Buxton's voice, thickened by the unwonted exertion: 'Move again and I'll break your ruddy arm'.

By the time I had found the switch that operated the other lights, the tableau was all set for the curtain. Buxton had Paul face down on the floor with his arm twisted behind his back, and Pat was still lying on the sofa in exactly the same position. Though she still smoked on, tears were trickling down her cheeks, making wet tracks through the makeup.

'Poor Paul,' she said, 'poor faithful Paul, my divine lover and dancing partner . . . Must you be so brutal, Inspector?

He's a gentle person normally. It's just that anybody who sees enough of me ends up by wanting to kill me. If there were any justice in the world, I would have got what he gave Annie.'

Paul was standing now, smoothing back his hair. He was massaging his arm, but he seemed more worried about his white tie, which he could see, in the mirror over the mantelpiece, hanging down like a broken cabbage-white. Buxton was examining the pistol. 'Two gone. Yes, I think we shall find this is the weapon that killed McBane.' He glanced at Paul and rapped out: 'Where did you change your clothes?'

'I didn't change my clothes. I had my Teddybear coat over my tails. You'll find it in the back of the car.' If he expected Paul to be difficult he was quite mistaken.

'Why did you have to kill Dugald and not me?' Pat's voice was gentle and she patted the sofa beside her in a strange, but very characteristic attempt to show Paul that she wasn't angry with him. 'Come and sit here, Paul.'

But Paul remained standing. He said: 'Because you looked so lovely, sitting up in bed with that gun in your hand; and I knew by then that he wasn't your man any more. I thought we might go dancing again, perhaps be partners professionally. I thought you might even love me when you knew I killed him. . . . Then I saw you kneeling beside his body, *kissing* him . . . and I thought to myself, let her think she did it, let the bitch suffer . . . ' Paul's face suddenly wrinkled up like a monkey's and he flung himself down at Pat's feet, kissing her shoes passionately.

Buxton and I looked the other way.

Cumberledge, torn between discretion and curiosity, had taken it on himself to bring chicken sandwiches and hock. He must have started making them soon after the shot went off. The glasses rattled together so loudly that he had to set the tray down quickly and exit no wiser than he had entered.

Buxton ate and drank with unhurried relish, despite the pointed yawns of his C.I.D. driver, who was sitting in a dark corner of the room waiting to take him back to London with his prize.

The atmosphere had become relaxed, almost friendly. Buxton, like all good detectives at the end of the hunt, was feeling benevolent towards his victim. And Paul basked in this benevolence: the ego that had been trampled into homicidal hatred was now flattered into a kind of euphoria. Only Pat supplied the continuity. Like me, though for different reasons, she was thinking of Dugald, the mystery man; whose mystery had been partly that of class, partly of sex and partly disillusionment. Perhaps she was remembering the romantic moment when he first accosted her on the ship.

Because of her, Buxton's insensibility grated on me somewhat. But I can't pretend that I thought worse of him. I too had a faint sense of triumph. Not only because I had served the cause of justice, but also because justice seemed to have served my cause. *The police had evidently seen nothing phoney about Mrs Van Dopp's suicide* ...

It seemed odd to be conducting – as it were – a post-mortem on a patient who was still alive. But Paul was the least embarrassed of us. He listened with keen interest, correcting us with a kind of childish pertness when we went wrong about a detail. When Buxton asked him what he had done with Mrs Tatham's jewellery, he suddenly had a fit of giggling.

'How much are they worth to you?' he asked.

'They're worth nothing to *you*.' Buxton rebuked him. 'Come on now, Latta, it'll make things easier for you if you tell us.'

'They're deposited in Lloyds Bank, Pall Mall, in the name

of Dugald McBane! All except the bracelet I threw into the bushes.'

Buxton scribbled in his notebook, tore off the leaf and passed it to me. There was only one word on it:

BROADMOOR

Buxton shut up his notebook with a snap of elastic.

'Well, Mortimer,' he said. 'You're still slightly in the red, but now I'm prepared to give you credit. Damn me if you haven't missed your vocation!' He could afford to be generous to another Old Carthusian. We had both been suckled at the same breast.

I said: 'I don't want any credit. I wouldn't have known, I swear I wouldn't, if it hadn't been for the scratch on his leg. Even then I wouldn't have suspected him of the other murders until he revealed his talent as a mimic. Then I realized he must have played the role of McBane trying to plant the weapon on the Rideouts. And I suppose he also impersonated Mrs Van Dopp, ringing up to destroy the alibi we had all given him such credit for preserving?' I looked at Paul and he smiled and nodded. He stretched out for the last chicken sandwich, opened it and gobbled up the chicken, putting the empty bread back on the plate with a look that seemed to say: 'You see what I mean?'

When he had finished, he inserted a long finger into his mouth and with a precise, almost delicate, flick of the nail extracted a bit of chicken fibre from his tooth. He was enjoying the impatience with which we waited and he took his time wiping his mouth and re-arranging his handkerchief in his breast pocket. Then he said: 'That's right, doctor. Go to the top of the class. I don't suppose I saw McBane more than twice in my life, but once was enough to get him taped. Not that it mattered really. I just had to sound Scotch and pull my ear when I was talking to the old woman in the pub. She was

the one I worked on – there were no flies on that old bag!...'
He paused for a moment, smiling vacantly ... 'What was I
saying?... Oh yes, any ham could have done that act. You
could sell anything to Mollie – she's a natural. The thing that
took brains was seeing to it that McBane didn't have a proper
alibi that night. Do you remember, Pat? Do you remember
what happened on Monday night?'

The top of Pat's face was hidden by her hand. She blinked
in the lamplight as she took her hand away and said: 'Monday? When was Monday?'

'Monday was the day we met in the Dive at Victoria and
discussed what to do about Vera. We also talked about Kenya
and I told you about that Mau Mau film. I told you you
simply *had* to take McBane to see it.'

'That's right. You said it was the last day and if we didn't
go that night we would miss it.'

'That's what I *said*. I knew you'd never bother to check
up. And then I rang up later to ask what show you were going
to, just in case I was free to join you.'

'I remember. Well, what of it?'

'The film was at the New Victoria, four minutes by bus
from Mollie's place. That was the night I went to Mollie's as
McBane in disguise. He could never have proved that he
didn't slip out of the cinema ...'

'But I would have *sworn* that he ...'

Paul stopped her with raised hand and outspread fingers.
Pat managed to add a feeble 'you mean?...' and was
stopped again. The words came out of him delicately dis-
jointed, uttered in a tone of poisonous sweetness:

'I mean, sweetiepie, that your word wouldn't have saved
anybody's neck. Not by Tuesday it wouldn't have, anyway.
By that time the Chief-Inspector knew you were in the house
the night of the murder. Now do you see what little Paul was
up to?'

I looked at Pat and wondered how much more she could take. But she was still perfectly calm as she said:

'Did I really turn you into such a venomous little snake, or was I always too dumb to live?'

That was the question nobody felt like answering. Buxton cleared his throat tactfully and looked at his watch.

'I think we'd better be getting along. The sooner we have all this down in writing the better . . .' He turned to me and added quietly: 'By the way, Mortimer, what did you mean just now when you spoke of "the other murders", in the plural?'

'Did I say that? . . . Are you sure? . . . Then it must have been a slip of the tongue.'

I saw the expression changing on Pat's face and winked at her desperately. But I was too late. The nervous reaction had been building up in her and the hand holding the glass began to tremble, white knuckles starting out as she tightened her grip. Suddenly she started to shake with laughter: 'I give up, David: you're so, so incredibly funny, I can't take any more!'

I said sternly: 'Control yourself. Try and remember where you are and what's happened.'

'I know just where I am and what's happened. That's what's so funny. For everybody else it's the moment of truth, but for the great Doctor Mortimer, it's the moment to start telling lies!'

'Pat, you're hysterical. Take it easy now and I'll go and get you something to make you feel better.'

'Oh, stop it, can't you.' Her eyes blazed at me and she hurled her glass into the grate, covering the hearthrug with glittering splinters. 'There you are! All smashed, all in bits. Come on, David, tell the Inspector about the other murder you tried to pin on Dugald. Does he know that she couldn't have killed herself? Does he know she took the trouble to sterilize the skin before she injected herself?'

I said quickly: 'The murder hypothesis did just occur to me. But later on I changed my mind about it. I thought it more likely to have been an accident. I remembered seeing the glass of whisky on the bar.'

'But you didn't think of mentioning that to me, when you wanted to persuade me Dugald was a murderer. Be honest, you Medic! Are you trying to spare my feelings? Or is it just that you've lost interest now there's no point in hating Dugald any longer?' She turned her back on us and buried her face in the sofa.

A voice croaked: 'I'll tell you.'

Everybody but Pat looked towards the door. Sally was standing there in her nightdress, swaying slightly and trying to steady herself against the doorpost.

'Sally, go back to bed at once. You're drugged.'

'Give me your hand, David . . . what's done cannot be undone.'

I looked at Buxton and shrugged my shoulders.

'My wife's walking in her sleep. All this has been too much for her, and on top of it she's been reading Shakespeare. She said she wanted to re-read Macbeth just to see if the play said anything new to her after being involved in a real-life murder situation. Actually she often quotes tags when she's just emerging from the subliminal. She's always been crazy about literature and she's apt to see herself in literary situations that are more real to her than any reality.'

Buxton growled: 'What's all this? Can't you let your wife speak for herself?'

Sally rolled rather than walked to the nearest chair, with a kind of invertebrate, pseudopod progression. She collapsed into it and lay there gazing at me through eyelids that were blue and swollen with sleep.

'Why do you make such faces? . . . I tell you, what's done is done . . .'

I said: 'Come to bed, Sally ... She's somehow got the idea in her head that *she* killed Mrs Van Dopp, by doctoring the morphine I gave her. It's possible she actually *thought* of ways of doing it. Mrs Van Dopp, of course, knew I had lied about the time McBane and Lady Killaloe left my house, and she thought she could blackmail me into giving her dope off the record.... Come on, Sally, let's go up to bed.'

'What's the use? ... Oh, to sleep like her, a poppied sleep!'

Paul couldn't contain himself any longer. He was out of it. His thunder was being stolen, and so unconvincingly. He waved a contemptuous hand at Sally. 'Who does she think she is, I'd like to know? She's raving mad. I killed Vera. *I* killed her because she saw me when I got home that morning and guessed I was a murderer. It was then or never – if I hadn't killed Vera as well, I would never have been allowed to go away, never. It was hell with her – don't you all understand? – hell.'

'How did you do it, boy?' Buxton spoke to him gently, and was rewarded by grateful response in the soft, Mediterranean eyes.

'Oh, it wasn't so difficult really. I often used to lie awake thinking just how to do it: so that when it came to the point I was all ready ... '

He paused and looked round to see if we were all attending, if anybody would try and guess. Nobody spoke and he chuckled to himself: 'I hid her dope just long enough to make her crazy. Then I found it for her among the spice bottles in the kitchen! By that time she wanted it so badly that she put it straight into the main line. And did she love me? Oh boy! ... "Come on, Vera," I said, "let's really go to town. Do you want to get a big bang?" "You little devil," she said, "what shall we do?" "I'll tell you what we'll do. I'll make one of

those big black Bacardis you're so sold on – if I haven't forgotten how to do it." . . . I hadn't forgotten. My Bacardi was
the tops. But instead of grenadine in the rum, she had a
whacking dose of some specially strong cough-syrup the
doctor gave me for my laryngitis. It was so full of heroin, you
weren't supposed to take more than a coffeespoonful every
four hours. She had nearly half the bottle – and boy! was she
skating? . . . Afterwards I washed out the inside of the glass
very carefully and left it in the bar with some neat whisky in
it – just to show where the alcohol came from! . . .'

We stared at one another in shocked silence – at least
Buxton and I did, because Sally and Pat were more or less
out of it, and the police-driver had never been in it. But Buxton got up and took Paul's arm. He was feeling very tender
towards him.

'We'll be able to dot the i's and cross the t's when we get to
London. But there's one little detail we ought to clear up
while we're still with the doctor. You say Vera wanted the
dope so badly she shot it straight into the main line. But
Doctor Mortimer says she sterilized her arm beforehand.
That doesn't make sense to me.'

Paul's face was working again; his mouth trembled and I
thought for a moment he was going to burst into tears. I was
wrong.

'I hate you all,' he screamed, 'I hate your stupid staring
eyes. Don't you understand that I can't be pushed around
any more, that I can't be played with?' He paused, then
sneered: 'I thought the police would have more intelligence.
I sterilized her arm after she went into her coma, just to make
sure the verdict would be Accidental Death . . . I couldn't
tell you to look at her arm, now could I?'

I took Sally to bed. She was still half asleep and I didn't
dare wake her up to ask the question that tormented me. But

I remembered that she had been in torment too, and I tucked her in and gave her a kiss.

'It'll be all right, now. Everything will be all right.'

She didn't know she heard me, but she turned over on her side and smiled.

Pat was still lying on the sofa, smoking. But she had combed her hair and repaired her face, and her morale was visibly higher for it.

'Goodbye,' I said. 'This is really goodbye. We shan't be seeing you in the morning . . . What are you going to do with yourself?'

She flashed me a ghost of her old social smile. She was nothing if not courageous.

'I was just thinking about myself . . . No, I don't think I'll commit suicide . . . Maybe I'll go back to Desmond for a while and live in that divine castle in County Limerick. Then you could come and stay with me for the fishing. You do still fish, don't you?'

'I've spent a week fishing in troubled waters, and as a result I've nearly lost Sally. No, I'll keep away from that divine castle, thank you. It might be haunted: and, besides, my tastes have become exclusively bourgeois.'

She shrugged me off and made a little non-committal gesture.

'Well, that leaves me with absolutely nothing but a clear field of action.' She looked up at me and wrinkled her nose. 'I think I'll go west and prospect for gold! *Tant pis!*'

Sally and I were driving back to London.

'Did you really tamper with that bottle of morphine?'

'Don't you believe I'm capable of it?'

'Answer my question, *please*.'

'No, you answer mine.'

'Well then . . . yes, I believe you could have done it – for *me*.'

Sally sighed with contentment: 'Actually I didn't do it. But I did take the tablets out and hide them, and I did forge the entry in the book, just in case it was necessary to keep up the fiction. You see, apart from wanting to get you away from Pat, I wanted to shock you into seeing me afresh, as Macbeth must have seen his wife afresh when he exclaimed. "Bring forth men children only!" '

'Maybe you've got something there,' I mused, 'I mean about bringing forth children.'

Another Penguin by James Byrom

OR BE HE DEAD

In delving into records of the 1890s, Raymond Kennington finds a fascinating case of murder and blackmail which he uses in the latest of his much-bought crime stories. But just before publication there is the awful realization that one of the men acquitted through lack of evidence may still be alive and would certainly sue for libel. Author, together with publisher's secretary, set themselves up as sleuths and get embroiled in a particularly exciting manhunt through London and the Paris underworld.

'The writing is admirably crisp and intelligent, and that difficult blend of past with present and violence with ratiocination is smoothly achieved' – Maurice Richardson in the *Observer*

'It is a great pleasure to welcome a crime novelist so lively and literate and undonnishly urbane' – Julian Symons in the *Sunday Times*

'James Byrom has most successfully combined a light-hearted, rather wry wit with a clever plot. This is an intelligent, amusing book' – *Birmingham Post*